Missing in Time

Second Edition
Published by Library Stamp
This Edition Published in 2019

First Edition Published 2012
Copyright © Catherine Harriott

ISBN-13: 978-1546892489
ISBN-10: 1546892486

All rights reserved.
No part of this publication may be reproduced, stored in a retrieval system, or transmitted in any form or by any means without the prior consent of the author, nor be otherwise circulated in any form of binding or cover other than that in which it is published and without a similar condition being imposed on the subsequent purchaser.

To reduce carbon footprints
the author will donate trees to the
Woodlands Trust
www.WoodlandTrust.org.uk

A portion of author royalties for this book will go to the following two foundations, one launched by Christopher Reeve the other by Michael J. Fox
two extraordinary time travelers
www.ChristopherReeve.org
www.MichaelJFox.org

ACKNOWLEDGMENTS

Thanks for their guidance
Sandra Glover: Writer/Teacher/Editor
Kathryn Price: Cornerstones Literacy

Much thanks to artist Natalie Yau
for her lovely drawing of Robin Hood's Bay
and Brumpton Manor House

Cover design by Robin Ludwig Design Inc.
www.gobookcoverdesign.com

PART ONE: JET LAG

Unlocking the Past	1
Upstairs	6
What's Happening?	11
Panic	13

PART TWO: BRUMPTON MANOR

Who are You?	16
Craziness	23
Rear Window	26
Brumpton Manor: The Movie	31
There's No Place Like Home	35
Empty House	41
Never-ending Day	44
Close Encounters of the Weird Kind	48
Escape	56
Adrian	61
Day Off	67
The Village	70
The Future or the Past?	74

Questions	76
Hard-knock Life	81
Trapped	87
Scenery Helps	92
Lost Days	96
New Day	99
The Calm	104
The Storm	107
Shining Light	113
Forgetting Where I Am	117
The Birds	121
Mr. Brumpton's Study	125
Missing Page	129
To Catch a Thief	134
Criss-cross	140
Spirited Away	145
Sunny Side	147
Discovery	150
Where You Going?	154

PART THREE: SHIP OF NIGHTMARES

Travel Plans	158
Two Days Left to Sail	162
Urgent News	166
Invisible Servant	168
Stressed	172
One Day Left to Sail	175
For Your Eyes Only	178
The Train	181
Get off the Train	185
Frustration	191
Not There Yet	193
No More Days Left	196
Messages	201
Warning	204
Last Chance	207
Arrested	212
Which Way?	214
First Class	216

Adrian's Back Story	218
Robin Hood's Bay	221
Crystal Power	225
Frantic	228
Tell Me	230
No More Time	236

LOVE TO

Kim who read this book first and had great insight and advice.

Sam an amazingly original thinker and writing buddy.

And H as we travel this planet together.

PART ONE

JET LAG

UNLOCKING THE PAST

It's late, but I'm wide awake in Aunt Dottie's basement, having a polite mug of tea with Gran, listening to the two of them catch up. I don't like tea, so I pretend to drink it.

Gran changes her watch to British time.

"You've travelled forward in time," Aunt Dottie says, gazing at me from under her modern red-framed glasses. In fact, except for her name, everything about Aunt Dottie is modern. From her sparkly blue sweater to her cut-off yoga pants. She hasn't let her hair go gray like Gran's either. It's a nice rich brown color.

And the house.

I don't know what the rest of it looks like, but this space-age kitchen in her basement surprises me. I mean, I thought everyone in England had flowery patterns and antique furniture. I listen to her rattling on in her British accent. She says words like aeroplane instead of airplane.

Cute.

I don't say much. I feel like I'm still up in the air on my first flight ever, among those white cotton-candy clouds.

Aunt Dottie tops up Gran's golden mug from the teapot and turns her swivel stool to face me. "You don't look like your mum," she says, "Or your dad."

I scrape my stool back from the kitchen bench and feel my face flush. I don't want her to mention my mom or my dad. That's private. Do not enter.

Aunt Dottie stares at my hair but speaks to Gran. "Zoe's hair wasn't this gorgeous reddy-brown color." She leans forward, examining me like a bug under a microscope. "Mmm, it's got bits of gold in it too."

I turn away and push my pain down. The way I always do when either of my parents are mentioned. They're both gone now. I can't talk about it.

So I study the night sky through the window and wonder what the view looks like in the day. Nothing like Orlando, that's for sure. No highway signs: Magic Kingdom this way, Universal Studios that.

"You look tired," Aunt Dottie says to Gran, and I turn back round. "Do you want to rest tomorrow?"

Gran smoothes down her seriously mixed-up red and purple dress, then brushes a hand through her gray hair that's standing up like Doc Brown's from *Back to the Future*. I'd probably find her look hilarious if I didn't have to go out in public with her.

"What d'you think, Sal?" Gran says. "How about a PJ day tomorrow?"

"What's a PJ day?" Aunt Dottie asks.

Gran coughs her nervous cough and looks at me. "You tell her."

"It's when I'm allowed to wear pajamas and hide from the world all day."

I don't tell her it's instead of an allowance.

"Sounds wonderful," Aunt Dottie says. "But I'd have thought you'd have been at those theme parks every day with your friends."

Friends? My movies are my friends. No one at school knows either. If they think it's weird I can't afford to go to the theme parks, I'm not about to tell anyone I buy second-hand movies, mostly from the black-and-white days.

"There's nothing like theme parks round here," Aunt Dottie points out. "But we can explore the village, if you like. Maybe catch a bus tour or two."

She swivels her stool back to Gran as if she's just thought of something. "Sally's never been here before. Shall I show her my photographs?" Without waiting for an answer, she slides off her stool, moves over to a cabinet, and taking a small key she unlocks a drawer and dumps a stack of brown-tinged photographs on the kitchen bench.

I try not to sigh. What is it about older people and their photographs? Gran's the same. Always trying to tell me stories about the past. Why keep dragging it up? Better to lock the past up and throw away the key.

"Look at this one," Aunt Dottie says, waving a photo in my face. "She fought for women's rights, you know."

I barely look but pretend to sift through the stack. One of the photographs drops onto the floor, and I pick it up.

It's of a girl standing in front of an old-fashioned bicycle shop with her hair blowing about. Her face is hidden by the shadowy imprint of someone's finger. The person behind the camera has ruined it. "Why even keep such a photograph?"

Oh no. Did I say that out loud?

Gran's pale shocked stare tells me I've gone too far this time.

"You know," Gran says, her hurt voice making me curl-up inside. "Every family photograph has a story behind it, even a ruined one."

I'm about to say I'm sorry, but Aunt Dottie quickly changes the subject.

"Now, I've sorted out a couple of bedrooms for you down here."

Down here? In the basement?

She turns back to me. "You'll see when it's light just how big this house is from the outside. But I don't want you going into any of the rooms upstairs. They're all closed-up, and some are half finished and not safe."

Her voice doesn't sound cute any more, just strict. And her eyes are cold when she shrugs at Gran. "Workmen, hey?" And Gran shrugs back, as if she's always ordering workmen around too.

"What're you doing with the house?" Gran asks.

Aunt Dottie passes us a plate of chocolate cookies.

"Nothing now," she answers. "I used to run a hotel, but what with everyone going abroad, I had to close up. The cottages in the village do well with weekenders, but no one wants to stay in a manor house like this without a lift."

I bite into a cookie, letting the rich chocolate melt in my mouth. "It'd be fun to explore," I say, more to Gran than my second aunt once removed.

"I'm asking you not to," Aunt Dottie answers in that strict voice again.

"She won't," Gran says for me.

I want to start arguing my case but Gran's mouth is set in a hard line. Mission impossible.

Though Aunt Dottie's face softens as she looks at me. "Help yourself to any films. They're in your room. Your gran told me you like Hollywood and such. I usually download mine but my service is out." She looks at Gran. "Typical, hey?"

Gran nods as if we even have downloaded movies. "Sally watches a movie before breakfast."

"My morning movie is like your coffee," I say, suddenly feeling the need to defend my life. "It wakes me up."

"Well, you're on holiday now," Aunt Dottie says, stopping our argument. "So like I said, help yourself."

"Thanks," I mumble.

I gaze round at all her shiny stainless steel appliances. We'd better not invite her back across the pond. Even our washing machine does a thumping dance on the spin cycle. Not to mention our dishwasher's kaput. But look over there — a flat-screen TV in the kitchen — awesome. "What's that?" I ask, pointing to a large opening in the wall.

"That?" Aunt Dottie says, looking over. "That's a dumbwaiter."

"Pop quiz: What's a dumbwaiter?"

Gran doesn't look up. She's used to me saying pop quiz to start a question.

But Aunt Dottie pauses as if I've said something foreign, before saying, "It's like a little lift for sending dishes up and down between floors. Very handy when I used to run the hotel. You just pull on the rope to make it go up or down." She turns to Gran. "It's bigger than they normally are. I was going to convert it to electric but, what with closing down the hotel, it didn't seem worth it."

"Does it still work?" I ask, my hands itching to go over and pull on the rope.

"I haven't used it in years," Aunt Dottie answers. "I think the rope's twisted."

I jump off my stool, ready to walk over to the dumbwaiter.

Gran coughs again and stops me. "Bed, I think, Sal."

Jeesh! She never lets me do anything.

But as I head for the kitchen door, I console myself with the thought that I'm here all week. Plenty of time to explore later.

UPSTAIRS

Passing the forbidden stairs, I pull my suitcase on wheels into the bedroom I'll be staying in. My five-star room, bathroom en-suite, has—get this—a whirlpool tub, complete with a row of fancy unopened shampoos, conditioners and bubbles. I'll definitely be soaking in that tomorrow.

Gran taps on my door. "Amazing house, eh?"

"You kiddin'? Not like ours."

Gran looks offended. "There's nothing wrong with our house."

Nothing wrong? Does she stay at the same address as me? Broken doorsteps, cracked walls. Tucked away in the woods all on its own without a neighbor in sight.

She hovers next to my suitcase. "You could have been nicer to your aunt."

"You know I don't like talking about the past."

"The past can be full of stories. Same as I told your mom." Her blue eyes have a sad, far-off look.

"Oh, Gran—"

"I know, I know," she says. "You can't turn back the hands of time."

I try to think of something nice to say, but she starts bugging me about keeping the room tidy.

I close my ears. I've heard all Gran's scripts before.

"Are you listening?" she asks. "I can't step on your floor at home without snapping old DVDs."

My movies may be in one big mess to Gran's picky eyes, but to me they're in organized, alphabetical stacks. Is it my fault that the stacks get kicked about a bit and spill into each other? I mean, what's her problem? I leave enough space to cross the room.

"Just remember, this isn't your home." Gran heads to the door. "Goodnight, then."

A goodnight hug is left hanging in the air between us. Tired of her lectures, I push the hug away as I push the door closed. I feel guilty immediately and open the door again, but she's gone.

Now I throw my suitcase on the bed, casting a quick glance at the corner bookcase filled with movies. I'm trying not to be mean, to be polite to my aunt and patient with Gran, and not be ashamed of our house. But I don't think Gran gets it. That this is my break from school where I always have to pretend my life is something else. Something better. Like everyone else in my class. That's why I need to hide in a movie.

But I should try and sleep in this time zone.

I unzip my suitcase and rummage through it, scattering socks and underwear and my thumb-stained copy of *One Hundred Years of Classic Movies*. I'm up to the Hitchcock chapter: 'Director of Suspense.'

The only thing I can find for sleeping in is this white cotton nightgown Gran bought for me with her pawn-store money. Yes, Aunt Dottie paid for our flights, but Gran had to sell a bunch of things so we won't be treated like charity cases in a foreign country.

I yank out the nightgown and make a face. Gran's got to be kidding me. This shapeless thing? And check out the old-lady lace on the sleeves and hem. She must think I'm a hundred or something.

But I pull the nightgown over my head anyway, and as I glide across the room, I have to admit, it does feel nice trailing the floor. Like one of those ladies from my movies in the black-and-white days.

Aunt Dottie's movie collection—how could I resist?—makes me feel right at home. She even has *Groundhog Day*. Now I've got my old favorite to watch if I can't sleep. I should be able to, though. It's lovely and Florida warm in here, what with the heating cranked up so high.

But when I climb into bed, I toss and turn, thinking about everything that's happened since last week. Last Saturday actually, when Gran announced that my second aunt once removed had called to say, I was going to England.

At first I was excited, especially when I'd looked over at the *Enchanted* calendar on the wall and seen February 10th circled. Half-term break. Only one week away. That meant Big Ben, London Eye, Leicester Square movie premieres here I come. But when I'd found out we were going to Yorkshire not London, Gran had seen my dropped-shoulder reaction and reminded me that she'd never been on a plane when she was at middle school.

And another problem.

Gran was coming with me.

The thing is, I've never had a mom since I was a baby, so Gran watches me like a detective. I suppose that's why Dad never let me do anything risky when he was alive. Once, four years ago last summer, before he was sick, I wanted to go on this trip with the class. We were going sailing on Lake Kissimmee, and he told me how to punch an alligator in the face in case I fell in. But he changed his mind and never let me go. It's hard to have friends if you can never do anything, and now Dad's gone and Gran has no money, so I still can't go anywhere.

OK, I decide, kicking off the heavy covers, even if I'm not in London, at least this is somewhere different. Going to England is different. And as Bill Murray says in *Groundhog Day*, anything different is good.

For a while I think about being on my first vacation ever and how flying was so exciting and how I'm in a foreign country and I can't wait to see it all tomorrow. The time slips by, and I still can't sleep. I try to read my book but I can't focus and keep reading the same sentence over and over.

May as well watch a movie.

There's no player in here, so I climb out of the cozy nest of my bed, throw my robe on, stuff *Groundhog Day* inside my pocket and head for the kitchen. Maybe I'll find a player in there.

I do feel a bit weird though, wandering around someone's house on my own, even if I am a relation. But I can't stare at the ceiling all night.

Flicking on the kitchen's bright lights, I notice a player on a shelf under the flat screen TV.

It's not hooked up.

On my way back to my bedroom I see the stairs and ask: What's the point of being here if I can't explore this big rambling mansion? This may be an amazing basement but it's still a basement. Anyway, blame it on the jet lag. Or the fact we don't have any stairs. But next thing, I'm on the floor above, opening doors.

* * *

The first room I try, I can't tell what it once was. All the furniture is covered in dust sheets, and there's a fireplace, half demolished.

But this next room looks like a hotel dining room, what with all these round tables and chairs and that long side table, probably used for putting dishes of food on. Oh, and there's the dumbwaiter. The little elevator in the wall. I go poke my head in. It's pretty big for just plates. It could hold a person if they scrunched up tight.

I'm about to touch the rope when I hear a noise on the stairs. Is Aunt Dottie coming? Or, worse, Gran? Gran's going to think I'm ungrateful. She'll want to keep track of me for the rest of the week. I've got to hide. I eye the room. But where? There are no curtains or dustsheets to hide behind in here. No cupboards to crouch in. The tables don't have tablecloths to crawl under. My eyes turn to the dumbwaiter. I hoist myself up and pull down the door.

Darkness closes in. It's like I'm sitting in a shaking box. I won't be able to stay more than a couple of knee-bending minutes. I try to keep steady, but my body feels too heavy, suspended here in the wall. I can't breathe. What am I thinking? I've got to get out of here. I lift the door up and strain to listen. I can hear a clock ticking. That's all. No one's coming. I'm about to move when a rumbling noise starts below my feet.

Bruce Almighty! Is the thing going to break and tumble to the ground?

WHAT'S HAPPENING?

"Help!" I call out.

I edge my way forwards. The dumbwaiter shakes and I'm pushed back. The dumbwaiter drops — I scream — and it stops as if my scream had commanded it to.

Now the dumbwaiter's stuck in the chute, and I'm clinging to the sides in scary blackness.

"Help!" I call out again.

Why doesn't Gran come? My heart's pounding. My palms are sweating. I'm afraid to move a single inch. If the dumbwaiter falls again I could trap my hands on the wall. I could *lose* my fingers. I could *lose* my toes. I curl up into the smallest, tightest ball and clench my teeth.

The dumbwaiter descends.

My stomach stays at the top but the rest of me falls. I'm in a Tower of Terror and I want this to end. But it doesn't end. What's happening? One minute I'm in my bedroom, now I'm falling in a dumbwaiter. Nightmare.

That's it! I'm having the most fantastical falling dream. It's the thought I cling onto as I reach out and try to hold on.

But now the chute isn't there any more, and I'm not going straight. I'm spinning and spinning and sparkling lights fly past.

At last the dumbwaiter slows—rises—stops with a jolt and—feet first—I
>   fall
>   out.

PANIC

I wait for the world to stop spinning, so I can run from Aunt Dottie's basement kitchen back to my room.

But this doesn't look like her kitchen.

Everywhere's full of dark shadows of every size and gruesome shape. I scream and grab onto the dumbwaiter. It feels harmless again—solid. I jump back in and hold on.

Nothing.

I shake the dumbwaiter, but I'm scared it might break, so I jump back down. My heart's racing; I can feel it thumping as I hunt with my eyes for the door. There are two: a closed one on my right and an open one on the far side.

But my feet won't move.

I'm sweating. But at the same time, I shiver.

Stay calm. Stay calm.

There's a dim light on the other side of the open door. It's spilling part way into the room onto hanging saucepans. Some as large as cauldrons. Where am I? A lower floor, perhaps? Dug under Aunt Dottie's basement. I stare at the open door. Above it I can see a row of bells. Why? Are they left over from her hotel? This is definitely not her kitchen. That big black stove wasn't in it. Or that rocking chair. I hold my breath.

It's empty.

My breathing starts again. This time too fast. I take a couple of cautious steps and bump into a table. Something rattles on it. Something heavy. I want to hold onto the table, but I daren't touch a thing. Footsteps. I hear footsteps. The room swims: the pans, the bells, the stove, the chair, start to fade. A buzzing noise. In my ears. Louder.

Everything goes black.

PART TWO

BRUMPTON MANOR

WHO ARE YOU?

My eyes flicker open. Something rough is licking my cheek. A black cat with a white spot across its nose. It leaves my side, pads across the stone floor and rubs against a pair of legs.

Raising my body off the floor, I look straight into the eyes of a curly-haired boy who's standing by the open door. He's holding a lantern. He lifts it higher and the light shines his hair.

"You fair flummoxed me, lying there like that," he says.

"What?" I try to stand but my limbs feel weighted down.

"Ye all right, lass?"

"Yeah," I lie. His lantern sways. I watch it, mesmerized. "Have you had a power cut?"

No answer.

"Where am I?"

"Robin Hood's Bay."

Is that where this is? I know I'm supposed to be in Yorkshire somewhere. "Who are you?" I ask.

He stands to attention. "Adrian Merryweather, first footman at your service." He moves in closer. "Who are you? Where did you come from? Did you fall over? That floor can be right slippy if our Gerty didn't get to it."

So many questions I don't have the energy to answer.

He strides over and holds out his hand. I don't know why, I reach up and take it—it feels warm and strong—and he helps me scramble to my feet.

Something about him makes me relax. I try to convince myself everything's all right. I just need to get back to Gran.

"Which way upstairs?"

"To the main house?" He glances at my robe. "You can't go up like that."

I'm about to demand a cell phone, but I don't know Aunt Dottie's number.

"What's thee name?" he asks.

"Sally. Sally Soforth."

"Where're you from?"

"I'm from"—I look back at the dumbwaiter—"from Orlando."

"Where's that?" he asks. "Down south?"

"Yes . . . down south," I reply, still staring at the dumbwaiter.

"Are you our new maid?"

I spin round. Maid? Me? The boy's dreaming.

Or is it me? Am I still in my falling dream?

"We thought you'd changed thee mind." He glances at my robe again. "Has anyone shown you your room?"

I shake my head.

"You'd better come wi' me; 'tis too late to meet t'others." His eyes search the floor. "Where's your tin trunk?"

"Trunk?"

"Is it being sent on?"

"Mmm," I say, and he takes that for a yes.

"You'll be needing a uniform. You're in luck, the last maid left hers; I'll fetch it." And he walks out the door, taking the light with him.

I move closer to the dumbwaiter and stare into it.

"That's our dumbwaiter." The boy's voice makes me jump.

He couldn't have been gone more than ten seconds. "'Tis bigger than your average, don't you think?"

"Yes, bigger," I say, absently. How did the dumbwaiter do that? It felt... it felt like how I imagine a theme-park ride would feel. A scary ride.

"It runs nice and smooth with that new rope we had fitted today." He presses a bundle of clothes into my hands. "There's even a pair o' shoes," he says, dangling by their laces not shoes, but a pair of black ankle boots. "Here, takes 'em."

Without thinking, I reach for the boots.

"Follow me," he says.

In a kind of robotic daze, I follow him out the room, my bare feet numb on the stone floor. We reach the beginning of a winding staircase. I snap out of my daze.

I won't climb it. I won't go one step further.

The boy swings round and his lantern swings too, making the shadows dance on the wall behind him. "Come on," he says. "'Tis all right."

Famous last words.

I glance over my shoulder, wondering if I should make a run for it back to the dumbwaiter. Or should I tear up the stairs and find Aunt Dottie's?

The boy's waiting. I study his face. He doesn't seem like the attacking type but you never can tell. He could be Dracula for all I know. But which is worse? Being alone in this power cut or taking a chance with this boy?

I nod, and we start to climb.

"I hope you stay," he says, as we reach a small landing. "We're like family here. Except for the butler. He can't stand us havin' a laugh. Mrs. Meadowcroft—that's our cook—is champion."

He talks about a butler and a cook. Calls me a maid. This must be some rich person's house I've landed in. Maybe a movie star's. "Who owns this place?" I ask, following as close as I can to his lantern as we climb the winding stairs.

"The Brumptons. Didn't they tell you?"

Brumpton? Brumpton? I don't know any famous people with that last name. Then again, I only watch old movies. Must be wealthy though, to afford servants. But where's Aunt Dottie's house gone? Perhaps this is the house next door.

"Do you know the lady next door?"

"Next door?" he asks, turning to glance at me. "Our neighbors are down the village. We're the only one with servants, mind."

"How many servants work here?" I ask, as we round yet another stair corner. Sweat's dripping down my neck and the back of my legs are begging me to quit. Bruce Almighty! Just how many stairs are there? They don't seem to bother the boy, though. He just keeps climbing and talking without missing a beat.

"I don't rightly know," he answers. He starts counting them on his fingers. "There's Abigail. She has two jobs: first housemaid—aye—as well as lady's maid to Mrs. Brumpton. Mrs. B. doesn't want another woman runnin' things so there's no housekeeper, like as not in other big houses . . ." On and on he babbles as we trek up higher and higher, with me trying to juggle the bundle of uniform.

At last we reach the top. I stop and hold on to the rail to catch my breath. I nearly drop the boots and the boy's eyes widen. My heartbeat slows and I peer down a dark hallway. What's happening to me? Why am I up here? I look back down at the stairs and have a *Vertigo* moment where they seem to zoom and spin up towards me.

"Hurry," the boy whispers.

I set off again. He takes me to a room at the end of a long hallway. What should I do? Run? I mean, you hear of people being locked up in rooms and . . . my mind won't let me finish the thought.

"There's no key," the boy points out, turning the door handle and holding his lantern up.

19

I take a couple of slow steps inside. The room has a low sloping ceiling with a tiny square window at the end of the slope. A single metal bed is pushed against the back wall. The bed covers are pulled tight and there's only one pillow. I turn round in the small space, ready to run.

"Home-sweet-home," the boy says. He's leaning on a chunky wardrobe straight out of the Narnia movies. "Here, put your uniform down."

I drop my bundle on the end of the bed. I didn't realize I was still holding it.

He places his lantern down on a dresser, next to a half-used candle stuck in a holder with an ear-shaped handle.

I stare at the candle.

The boy follows my gaze. "I'll light thee candle for ye, but remember to blow it out. No gas up here. Mrs. Brumpton says we don't need it."

Lanterns, candles, gas. These people are the most organized ever for power cuts.

"Electrical generator?" I ask, thinking if they're this organized they must have an emergency generator somewhere, the way people do when a hurricane blows in. Perhaps this Brumpton guy is trying to get it going. On second thoughts, he's probably sending one of his servants to do it.

"Electricity?" the boy says with a laugh. "Folks round here still think yon train's newfangled."

Why does he keep saying thee and yon? Is he practicing for a part in one of Mr. Brumpton's period movies? He probably wants to get discovered. And who can blame him if he's a servant. He lights the stumpy candle. The small flame flickers, nearly drowning in its own wax. A single thought drips into my head and sends a shiver right through me.

Is he a ghost?

And now I look at him.

I *really* look at him.

His jacket has three silver buttons down each side. His collar is chin-high and creases over at the corners into little triangles. And he's wearing a bow tie. Why hadn't I noticed that before? I mean, just look at him. Apart from that dog-eared book sticking out of his left pocket, he could be going to a wedding. All he needs is a white carnation in his buttonhole.

Nothing is real. Nothing is real.

I shiver again. But is the boy real? Is this house haunted? Have I stumbled across the spirit world?

"Mind you," he says. "Bay's always last to get new fangled things. You won't find folk round here with a motorcar."

He smiles. A warm, natural smile that lights up his whole face. I don't think a ghost could do that. And now I think of it, his hand felt warm when he lifted me up. Ghosts can't lift people up. Can they?

"Aye," he adds. "You'd think in 1912 we'd get same inventions as yon city."

"What?"

"We can't get inventions. Master has as many as he can without electricity and—"

"The year. What year did you say?"

"1912."

"1912," I repeat.

"Aye."

"No."

"Aye. You sure you're all right?" He stares at my head.

"I'm fine." I touch my scalp and feel for a bump.

The boy pulls from his chest pocket a golden watch, dangling on the end of a long chain. After first checking to see if I'm looking, he flips open the lid. "'Tis late," he announces and snaps the watch shut. "The butler would have me hide if he knew I was up here."

He lifts his lantern off the dresser. "I'll ask Abigail to see you in the morning," he says, lowering his voice at the doorway. "She'll show you ropes—hey, what're you doing up here?"

The black cat, who'd licked me awake downstairs, is peering up at me. The boy scoops it up with his free hand. "That's the first time I've known Smudge leave our quarters."

Carrying the cat, he goes to walk away, but changes his mind and turns back round and whispers, "Can I ask ye a question?"

I hold my breath. He's realized I'm not a maid. A maid from 1912. I shake my head. That can't be the date.

"If you haven't got your tin trunk, where'd you get your night things from?" He glances at my robe.

"Um...from my bag," I answer, hoping he won't ask me where I've put my clothes or this missing bag.

"Oh." He looks at my empty hands, then back at my eyes. "Anyroad," he whispers. "Welcome to Brumpton Manor."

CRAZINESS

I close the door and lean against it. What just happened? I hold my hand over my mouth. I can't believe this. I must be still dreaming, and if I'm not, and it's true this is 1912, does Aunt Dottie know that her dumbwaiter transports people to another time?

No. Impossible. Crazy.

I let out a breath, and cross the wood floor. It's on a slant and creaks. I lift the candle lamp off the dresser. The light flickers. My hand's shaking.

Should I wait before I find my way back? I don't want to, but I picture the mountain of stairs and how dark they'll be without the boy's lantern, even with a candle to guide me. And who knows who's roaming the house. I might bump into one of those other servants. Or this Brumpton guy. No. I won't leave. Not until it gets light. That's when I'll escape.

But this means I'll be waiting all night. Alone. Should I try to sleep? Oh, Gran, where are you?

My legs feel weak, and I want to sit down. So I tug back the top bed cover to inspect the sheets with the candlelight as if I'm in some sort of scary motel. Except for sewn-up patches here and there, they're spotless. So I rest on the bed, tuck my knees under my chin and stare at the uniform.

What'll I do if I can't find Aunt Dottie and Gran? My stomach tightens at the thought of meeting more people.

People from 1912.

No. I don't believe it. One minute I'm in a basement with Gran and Aunt Dottie. A basement that's all bright and modern. Then I fall down a dumbwaiter to here. Is this some sort of a reaction to my jet lag? Perhaps I'm allergic to flying.

The candle flickers. Remembering what the boy said, I blow it out.

Stupid, stupid, stupid.

Now I'm in the dark and don't have anything with me to re-light it. I try not to panic. I hate the dark. I always leave my Pixar lamp burning all night. I blink my eyes, trying to see. Something else is missing. What is it? I listen.

That's it. No noise. None in the room, none coming from below. No sound of motors — no heating, no air conditioning, no ceiling fan — nothing. Just dead silence. It's hard to breathe with all this nothingness going on.

And impossible to sleep.

I wonder what time it is? I should've asked the boy. Adrian. Funny how I remember his name. Has Gran missed me yet? How long have I been missing? An hour at the most. I cup my chin in my hands. Why did that dumbwaiter do that? Why did it bring me here? But where's here? Perhaps I can see out the window.

I scramble out of bed in the dark and bang my head on the ceiling. "Ooh," I moan. I'll have to watch that.

But the pain slows my brain down and makes me ask — did I hurt myself falling down the dumbwaiter? Am I lying unconscious on Aunt Dottie's floor, hallucinating the whole 1912 thing?

Come on, wake up, wake up.

But I don't wake up. I'm still here.

Pushing away every instinct to go screaming out the room, I feel my way towards the window in the dark. I kneel down and press my nose to the glass. But the moon's covered in thick clouds. I can't see a thing in the black night. I stand up and shuffle back across the room, careful of the ceiling this time.

One last thing. I go pull open the door.

"Aunt Dottie!"

Silence.

There's nothing to do now but hide under the bed covers, blank everything out and wait.

REAR WINDOW

I rub the terrible nightmare from my eyes. Yay! First day of vacation. I clutch the blanket round my shoulder. Brrh, but England's cold. This bed's lumpy too. I stare up at the ceiling. It slopes. My eyes dart round the room and last night comes flooding back in one big horrible rush.

Oh no! My nightmare's real.

My head starts to buzz, and I have to take deep breaths. At least it's light now. Though everything looks and feels so weird. So foreign. I almost laugh. I'm supposed to be on vacation. The first vacation of my life. Nothing makes sense.

Still clutching the blanket I climb out of bed and take small steps towards the window. I have to kneel to see out. The glass is misty. I blow cloudy breath on it but it doesn't clear. Ice has formed on the inside! How's that even possible? Why doesn't someone turn on the heat? I scratch at the glass, making ice slivers fall to the floor. Is this the view from my aunt's house?

Far below I see a frosty backyard with a winding footpath. A brick wall surrounds the yard. At the back is a wooden gate. Over the gate is a narrow trail. I follow it with my eyes as it slopes off, down to a tight cluster of red-roofed cottages all grouped in a circle next to—the sea.

There's a knock on the door. My legs wobble as I stand. I tell myself it's not because someone could be from 1912 waiting on the other side, but because I've had a restless night.

I pull open the door, take a few steps back, and in breezes a girl of about sixteen or seventeen in a long maid's outfit. A frilly cap tops her blonde hair.

"I'm Abigail. It's Sally, isn't it?" she says, and the sound of her voice breaks the quiet of the house. "Adrian just told me."

I notice I can understand her accent a lot easier than the boy's. Partly because she says each word deliberately as if English were her second language.

She glides over to the bed and straightens out her long white apron. "I'm first housemaid here," she says, sitting down on the edge. She starts picking imaginary bits of fluff off her sleeve. "I'm also on trial as Mrs. Brumpton's lady's maid, so I won't be able to give you much help with the floors and fires." She stops picking her sleeve and looks up at me, shrugging as if to say, "Hey, it's not my fault."

I feel like she's waiting for me to say something, but all I can do is give her a smile. Not a proper smile, just a left-side-of-the-mouth twitch.

"This your first job?" she asks.

I nod.

She shakes her head, making the frills on her cap flutter. "You don't know anything about being in service?"

Whatever she means, I know the answer is no.

For a split second she frowns.

I start shaking, partly with the cold, partly because I need the bathroom.

"Don't worry. You'll soon catch on." Abigail nods. "You can follow me around."

She pats the bed, suggesting I should sit down, and she starts going on about how the last maid left to get married. I try to pay attention but something in my head feels like it's slipping. I clutch at the bed covers. Am I really here? — I glance over at Abigail — she seems real enough, her blonde hair smells of lemons, and I can feel her boot touching mine, but she looks like an actress from the black-and-white days.

Wait!

In a flash, I think of a way to get me through this ... this nightmare. Until I can find a way back to Aunt Dottie's place and Gran, I'll pretend that I'm on a movie set and all the people — this maid, the boy from last night and any others I have to meet — are the characters. What's this place called? Brumpton Manor. That's it. I'm on the movie set of *Brumpton Manor*.

I let go of the bedcovers.

And tune into Abigail's voice. "If you need the WC, it's at the end of the hall."

"WC?"

"You know — water closet."

I've no idea what that means. A closet full of water? It doesn't make any sense.

Abigail stands, avoiding the low ceiling. "Time to get a move on." She unties her long white apron and reties it. "Oh, and we all go to church later if you want to come."

I follow her out the room. I don't want her to leave. "Just stage fright," I mumble to calm myself.

"What's that?" Abigail turns round. "There's nothing to be frightened of, Sally."

I can't handle her being kind again, so I shut my emotions off. I focus on my movie and — Abigail — the actress standing in the square of hallway under a skylight. The spotlight it casts, brightens me a bit. I take in the rest of the set: HALLWAY OUTSIDE MAID'S ATTIC ROOM. A table tucked inside an alcove, folded sheets piled on it next to a clock. The hallway narrows and stretches down to where the staircase is. Apart from closed doors on either side, there's nothing else for the cameraman to film.

"Right," Abigail, the actress, says. "I'll meet you in the servants' dining room in"—she glances at her watch and drops her precise speech for a second—"'ecky-thump, half-an-hour." And with a soft rustle of her uniform, she glides down the hallway and is gone.

"And scene," I hear the director of my movie say.

* * *

The first thing I do is try the end door. To my relief I discover a big toilet with a dangling chain, learning my first lesson on the movie set of *Brumpton Manor*. "A WC is the washroom," I say in my head.

But I don't really care what the rooms are named, I decide. I'll soon be out of here and it won't matter.

Back in the attic room, I lay out the maid's uniform, pretending I've just collected it from the wardrobe department. I scoop up a pale lilac dress and hold it against me.

And drop it.

I run to the door, scratching at the handle, ready to search the house for Gran or Aunt Dottie or, if this really is 1912, find the dumbwaiter to get me out of here.

I stop.

Way too risky.

I go pick the dress back up and force myself to hold back the ripples of panic that keep threatening to attack. Wearing this uniform will help get me into the part.

But it takes me ages to dress. There are lots of tiny buttons to fiddle with. The dress fits me—sort of. The waist's too small, and the hem doesn't quite reach my toes. I step into the boots. They pinch. I fasten the laces loosely and check myself in the dresser mirror. My auburn hair looks all wrong hanging over my shoulders. I twist it in a knot and push it under the cap. Umm. It looked much better on the other girl—I mean—actress. Abigail.

It's weird, though. Cap or no cap, the uniform gives me the courage to open the door and walk down the hallway.

But at the winding stairs, I hesitate. This is hard. The hardest thing I've ever done. But what other option do I have? So I grip the rail with one hand, my churning stomach with the other, and start to descend.

After one spiral of stairs, I come to a window that—like the skylight in the hallway—I never noticed in the dark last night. Below is a roof with a clock on it. No ocean view on this side. Stretching out are fields, rising gently up and down.

At the next window, I look down and see a horse! A man's leading it by the reins. I watch until they both disappear inside the building with the clock.

A leafless tree branch touches the next window. I hold back the urge to open the window and climb down and escape.

More steps to another window, then another. Each landing window brings me closer to the place I'm dreading, so each window gives me an excuse to stop and study the view.

But now there are no more windows and no more stairs. Just the boy from last night.

Adrian.

He's leaning against the stair post, his head bent as he fiddles with his watch, opening and closing the lid. He glances up and smiles that smile again.

"Breakfast," he says.

And we walk the lighted passageway ready, I try to convince myself, for my grand entrance.

BRUMPTON MANOR: THE MOVIE

The dining room's filled with people (I mean, actors) wearing uniforms, sitting around the most scratched table I've ever seen.

Definitely not Aunt Dottie's basement, then.

At the doorway, I watch over Adrian's shoulder as a small, motherly looking woman staggers into the room from another entranceway, carrying a huge teapot. She places it heavily on the scratched table and the black cat from last night, lying stretched out on the floor, glances up for a second.

"This is Sa—" Adrian starts to say.

"Merryweather!" A mean looking, thin-faced man standing at the head of the table growls in a low voice. "Go fetch the breakfast things or I'll knock you into next week."

"I was just going to, Mr. Birkett, but—"

"I find that difficult to believe," the man scoffs. He points a long finger at a pale girl with dark shadows under her eyes. "You, up!" he commands, but still in his weird, low voice.

The girl jumps out of her chair as if she's being yanked out of it by her maid's cap.

Adrian follows her out the room, leaving me standing alone, hiding halfway behind the door.

My nerves play with my senses, and the group at the table appear magnified. One by one they swivel their heads in my direction. I want to shout, Action! And almost do, but Adrian returns, carrying a huge platter of sausages, and he trips, nearly dropping the lot, and this calms me a bit.

The silence is broken by a man with intense black eyes, saying, "Who's this, then? Nay one tells me nowt." At the same time, the woman and the pale girl return, carrying more breakfast food.

"This is Sally, our new maid," Adrian announces. "She got here late last night." And as an afterthought he adds, "She comes from down south."

"She's a foreigner, then," the dark-eyed man mumbles.

"She's from Southampton—that's why she talks funny."

I do a double take. What made Adrian say that?

The mean guy throws him a nasty sneer. "You should have informed me last night, no matter how late the hour." He's almost whispering now, and the others lean forward, straining to listen. "Here, girl," he commands.

I nearly turn and run but find myself being bullied into the room, just by his eyes and body language.

"How come I wasn't informed of your arrival? I—"

The motherly woman interrupts him. "Let the lass through the door, Mr. Birkett." She points to a space at the table between Adrian and the pale girl. "Sit there, lass." She passes down a cup. "I always say there's nowt like a good cuppa tea at breakfast. Now, don't be shy, we only have till half past."

And Adrian takes out his pocket watch and flips open the lid.

The motherly woman hands a cup of tea to the mean guy. "The mistress has gone and hired her, Mr. Birkett. Like as not she told you, and you forgot."

The Birkett guy gasps. "I never forget anything Mrs. Brumpton tells me, Cook." He throws his harsh gaze around the room. "Let's get on." He lowers his head, and with a solemn voice says, "For what we are about to receive..."

And I'm sure I hear Adrian say under his breath, "The pigs have just refused."

Plates get passed down with sausages and sunny-side-up eggs on them. I hate eggs done this way. There's usually a runny bit on top. I take my fork and pretend to eat.

"Your water, Adrian," the motherly woman says, passing down a glass.

The pale girl next to me leans close and whispers in a shocked voice, "Adrian doesn't like tea." She looks at him as if he's breaking the law or something.

"What's your full name, girl?" Birkett asks, making me jump.

"Sally Soforth."

"Sally Soforth, Mr. Birkett," he corrects.

I feel my face tingle as everyone stares. "Sally Soforth, Mr. Birkett."

"I realize," he says, "that in the interests of economy we do not have a white tablecloth, but that is no reason to forget our manners now, is it?" He doesn't wait for my answer. "Have you your character? Or has Mrs. Brumpton got it?"

The seconds tick by as everyone waits for my reply.

Adrian jumps to my rescue. "She's come straight out of school, Mr. Birkett."

Birkett raises his voice ever so slightly, saying, "No one asked you." He glares at me, oozing disapproval. "It's most irregular that I wasn't informed." He pauses. "However, since you're here . . ." And he starts going round the table, introducing the other servants.

But I can't take it in. There are too many names to remember. Too many strange sounding jobs. Who cares, though. I'll soon be out of here and it won't matter if I remember them or not.

As Birkett drones on, Adrian takes his fork and starts carving something into the ridge of the table, shielding his work with his other hand. "Likes the sound of his own voice," he mumbles to me under his breath.

"Boy!" Birkett snaps. "Don't talk while I'm talking—and flatten your hair down or I'll take a carving knife to it."

Adrian tries to flatten his curls. He crosses his eyes at me, and he looks so ridiculous that I have to stifle a giggle.

"Quiet!" Birkett says, raising his voice without shouting, though it feels like he is. *How does he do that?*

Adrian leans back on his chair. I look down at the table. S-A-L, I read. He's carving my name! I look round to see if anyone else has noticed. The man who'd called me a foreigner stares at me with his dark, deep eyes. I look away, afraid he'll guess I'm acting.

"Right," Birkett says, "I suggest we all hurry up."

"Aren't you going to introduce Gerty, Mr. Birkett?" Adrian asks, looking at the pale girl with dark shadows under her eyes.

"No," Birkett says without looking up from his plate. "Now eat."

What a place!

And the people—I mean, the characters—so weird! Especially this Birkett guy. Pity these people having to work for him.

The black cat moves under the table and starts playing with my laces. I try to stay focused but my head feels floaty. Oh no, I'm not going to faint again, am I? I take a deep breath and look longingly over at the end doorway. I think it leads to that room I was in last night. Where the dumbwaiter is.

Adrian nudges my arm and nods at Birkett who's staring at my plate. I start eating. Everything looks different, smells different, tastes different. I could never get used to this place.

Never.

THERE'S NO PLACE LIKE HOME

A tinkly bell rings out from the direction of the kitchen. Birkett makes a big fuss leaving the dining room and everyone scatters.

I stare at the doorway, wondering if I'll get the chance to search for Aunt Dottie's place now. But Abigail catches my eye. She hands me a wooden box with a handle and a lift-out tray. The box is filled with brushes, dusters, cans and other stuff used for cleaning.

She takes me down a depressing hallway with brown-painted walls, up four worn-down brown stone steps, and like Dorothy, I open the door and my world turns to color — rich red velvet drapes, golden rugs, green plants, sparkling crystal chandeliers — and not a drop of brown paint in sight.

"This is the Brumptons' part of the house," Abigail announces.

But I don't have much time to take it all in before she starts explaining all my duties. To help me concentrate, I tell myself I'm doing some background research for my movie. Abigail begins to look at me funny though, when I keep asking her too many questions, so I just watch and listen.

The house is massive — there's no sign of Aunt Dottie's anywhere — and the rooms have names I've never heard of, like morning room and drawing room. Every one has a fireplace. Some are glowing.

"The worst part," Abigail explains in her precise voice, "is dragging up buckets of coal all day."

I don't tell her, I'm glad it won't be me carrying it up.

"The girl before you said that's why she left to get married." Abigail gives a half-laugh. "But I reckon it was 'cos she had to send all her wages home."

We walk side-by-side up a wide staircase, and my boots slip softly and smoothly on each thick-carpeted step.

"But," Abigail adds. "Now she's the clever clogs, training to be a typewriter. Getting all her evenings off."

I don't understand how a person can train to be a machine, but I keep quiet.

Abigail chatters on about the last maid until we reach a bedroom with pink stripy wallpaper. The fire's lit, making the room look cozy.

"You light the bedroom fires first thing," Abigail says. "When you're done, take the dead cinders down to the kitchen and put them in the stove—Mrs. Brumpton doesn't like waste." Abigail scoops up a bucket topped with a wire mesh and hands it to me. "There now, you're all set with your maid's box and cinder pail."

Just call me Cinderella.

She shows me how to make the bed properly, tucking the sheets in with square corners, then sends me away to make the next room's bed up.

Easy.

But tiredness isn't the right word to describe how I'm feeling right now. More like sleepwalking. So when I pull up the crisp white sheet under the soft plump pillow, the bed looks so inviting, I want to crawl inside it and sleep all day.

One little minute wouldn't hurt.

"Sally, Sally, what on earth are you doing?"

"Uh? What? Is that you, Gran?"

"No, it's not your gran!" Abigail shakes me.

I drag myself up.

"Go wash your face. If Birkett'd found you, it would have been the road for us both."

"Pop quiz—I mean—where do I wash-up?"

"Wash-up? Stop babbling. Gerty washes the dishes." Abigail glances nervously at the door. "Use Mrs. Brumpton's basin. Hurry, she'll be in from her walk with the dogs soon."

"Dogs? What dogs?"

"Mrs. Brumpton's dogs. Now move."

I stagger across the bedroom, pour water from Mrs. Brumpton's rose-colored pitcher and splash my face awake while Abigail remakes the bed.

"Why doesn't Mrs. Brumpton use her bathroom?" I ask, drying my face on my apron. I get the feeling I shouldn't use the plush pink towel hanging there.

"She likes her bedroom. It's warmer."

I straighten my apron and follow her into the hallway.

"Dusting," Abigail says, as I try to keep up with her on the Brumptons' stairs. "You do the drawing room. I'll do Mr. Brumpton's study. It's piled high with inventions and he doesn't want them disturbed, so you won't be allowed in there." She pauses for a second to pick out a can from my box. "Use this beeswax on the woodwork."

Phew! This movie's getting to be hard work.

But Abigail doesn't notice my exhaustion. She just ushers me into a room crowded with furniture and figurines.

"Right. Don't touch the gramophone records." She nods her head, looking proud. "Shame there's no electricity. But what can you expect when you live back-of-beyond." She checks both ends of the hallway before poking her head back into the room. "And watch out for Mr. Birkett's pennies; he hides them to catch us out and woe betide anyone who doesn't hand them in."

Why doesn't that surprise me? I'm alone now and taking

a moment to catch my breath. This Birkett guy's a real pain, and the girl who gets this job is in for a terrible time.

Ah well, back to my movie.

Using the beeswax, I polish anything made of wood. It's a fiddly job because I have to keep lifting figurines and other ornaments. Halfway through cleaning a bookshelf, I stop to flip through a magazine: *Edison Monthly*. Inside are illustrations of different types of big music players (no IPods here). One of them is even in this room. It has a huge horn sticking out of it shaped like a massive flower. I go over and give it a quick wipe with my cloth. Now I pull up the lid and see a turntable with a shiny black disk about the size of a dinner plate on it. This must be one of the records that Abigail told me not to touch.

Wow, it's heavy.

The player has a small wheel on the side. I place the record back onto the turntable and turn the wheel. No music comes out. So I drop the lid down and start polishing a nearby side table. Sensing something, I look up.

Birkett's standing there, looming in the doorway. "Well, get on with it," he says in his creepy low voice.

I try not to look in his direction as I work away.

"No, no, no," he rants. "Remove those ornaments first."

I clear the table, polish it, and move on to a chair.

"No, no, girl. That chair has legs."

The more he watches me, the more I rush, until a tiny finger from a lady figurine snaps off in my hand. I quickly drop it into a nearby plant.

"Finished?" Birkett snarls, luckily too far away to notice. "What's wrong with that bookshelf?"

"I did it before you came in . . . Mr. Birkett." I remember to say his name just in time.

"I find that difficult to believe. Did you remove all the books?"

My expression tells him I didn't. Why do I have to waste time cleaning things that are clean? This job makes no sense.

"There's a right way of doing things," he says. "And a wrong way."

He waits while I pull all the books off the bookshelf. I have a moment of looking outside of myself. Looking down from the ceiling at the girl frantically pulling books onto the floor. What is going on here? What crazy world am I living in?

But Birkett is watching, so I keep working, and when I'm finished I turn to see him pulling on a white glove with all the concentration of a surgeon. He strides over, sniffs, and I watch him as he runs a gloved-finger over every single surface.

The man's pathetic and needs to get a life.

* * *

Abigail finds me, but I don't tell her about Birkett. She already thinks I'm useless; why give her something else to worry about?

"I'll teach you tomorrow how to use the new rug cleaning invention Mr. Brumpton bought for me."

Tomorrow?

Tomorrow I won't be here.

"It's called The Wizard. You work it," Abigail explains, "by turning a wheel on the side." She places her hands on her incredibly narrow waist and shakes her head. "It's not very magical, though."

We head for the Brumptons' stairs. "That's it for Sunday morning," she says. "You coming to church?"

I forgot it was Sunday. It doesn't feel like a Sunday. I peer out of a side window. Two wide gates open onto a meadow with black crows circling the air. Go outside? In 1912? Way too scary. "I'll take a rain check."

"No need, it's not raining."

I try again. "Maybe next time."

"Well, if you're not coming, Mrs. Meadowcroft will want you to keep an eye on the roast."

We walk side-by-side down the Brumptons' wide staircase.

"Is everyone in the house going?" I ask, gripping the rail to stop me slipping. "I mean, will I be the only one left in the house?"

Abigail holds a duster to the rail as she goes down the stairs. "Everyone. Mrs. Brumpton insists we all wear our Sunday-best." She catches a glimpse of her face in the hallway mirror. "I think she enjoys showing us off."

"Even, Birk—I mean, Mr. Birkett?"

Abigail smirks as she pats her blonde hair. "Him. He never misses church."

* * *

On her way out of the kitchen, in a flowery hat that's seen better days, Mrs. Meadowcroft asks me to baste the meat every fifteen minutes.

"What does baste mean?" I ask her.

"Surely you aren't serious, lass?" She looks at my face. "Right, I can see you are. Just spoon melted fat over the meat or it'll dry up like a horse's saddle." She pulls on a pair of black gloves. "Which reminds me, don't let the roly-poly pudding pot go dry." She glances at the kitchen clock. "Eee, look at the time and me going on. Now, you'll be all right, lass, on your own?"

"I'm used to being home alone, Mrs. Meadowcroft."

Besides, I think, fixing my eyes on the dumbwaiter, I have my own plans.

EMPTY HOUSE

Coats, gloves and hats are collected and doors banged shut as everyone leaves for church. With the house to myself, I jump into action like a sprinter off the starting block.

I'm going back!

First, I run round the whole basement, double-checking for any sign of Aunt Dottie's. I swing open doors—to rooms, to cupboards—up one corridor, down the next. The stone floor echoes with my running steps.

Aunt Dottie's place is definitely not down here.

Ignoring the servants' stairs, I race to the end of the basement and scramble up the stone steps that lead to the Brumptons' part of the house. I'm hunting for their dining room. The second door I try, I find it. I head straight to the dumbwaiter and sit in it for as long as my legs will allow.

Nothing.

Maybe it'll work in the kitchen.

I hurry down the stairs, no longer thinking about movies or pretending to be in one. I'm totally focused now on getting back to Gran.

In the kitchen, I sidestep the table, reach out, grab hold of the rope, pull the dumbwaiter down and climb in.

Again, no luck.

Five times I sprint up the stairs. Five times down. On the sixth run up, my right boot slips off and, face down, I slide, scraping my shin on the way down. I pound the last step with my fists.

A loud bell rings. I stop and listen. It's not the same sound as the kitchen bells. It's coming from a box on the wall. I think it's a telephone.

I'm not answering that.

But it warns me that someone could come back any minute and find me here. So I hobble to the kitchen and flop down on the rocking chair to inspect my sore leg. The skin's peeled over a purple lump. I try to pat the lump and skin down but give up and lean back on the chair.

Backwards and forwards I rock. Backwards and forwards.

The pudding on the stove hisses. I hunt with my eyes for an escape, taking in the scrubbed kitchen table, the row of bells above the door, the gaslights, the hanging pans, the big black stove.

This is reality. Not a movie.

A spitting noise comes from the stove, reminding me I must see to the meat. I lean over and curl my hand over the oven handle. "Ow, ow, ow!" White blisters bubble up. Waving my burned hand in the air, I reach over with my other hand and snatch a dish towel off the table. The towel whips a glass bowl and it falls, smashing into a thousand pieces on the stone floor. At precisely this second, the pudding decides to erupt like a volcano, sending jam and pudding up the wall. I'm now in a crime scene in the middle of a horror movie.

"I can't do this!" I scream. "I can't!"

Loud sobs wrench at my body. "Gran, where are you?" I call; my voice pitiful, hollow. The black cat slinks over, nuzzling his head against my skirt. I lean down and stroke his silky fur.

When a door closes, somewhere a window opens.

It's a line from a movie. *The Sound of Music*, I think.

Well, I hope it's true. That there's a purpose to this craziness.

But what if the dumbwaiter is closed to me?

No. I refuse to believe it. I find a broom and, bit-by-bit, sweep up the broken bowl. Throw away the pieces. Get back into the part.

And when the others walk through the door, I'm surprised how glad I am to see Adrian's friendly face.

NEVER-ENDING DAY

Mrs. Meadowcroft whips up a vanilla dessert to replace the exploded roly-poly pudding. Gerty cleans the wall and drops the sticky remains outside the kitchen door into what she calls a slop bucket. Ned, the gardener, takes it to the compost to hide the evidence. Birkett's nowhere in sight. But I worry about the meat. I keep checking the bells on the wall, expecting the Brumptons to ring for the person who has ruined their lunch.

The bells stay quiet.

At two-thirty we all sit at the scratched table for our own lunch. I push my food round my plate. The others don't seem to notice. Except for Adrian who keeps glancing at me with a frown on his face.

When we're finished, I have to help Gerty clear the table, then Abigail tells me to go sort out the linen cupboard to check for anything that needs mending. A slow job with only one good hand. After about half an hour, I see Adrian walking towards me, but Abigail taps me on the shoulder and he darts out of sight.

"It's nearly four," she says.

I finish folding a napkin with an embroidered B in the corner. "That was a long day."

Abigail shakes her head. "At four we make the tea, and I leave it in the drawing room on a tray or serve it, depending on whether Mrs. Brumpton's entertaining her friends or not."

I collapse onto a nearby wooden chair and pull off my cap. My hair falls over my face. I let it hang there.

"Here, take these," Abigail says in a kinder tone, placing two hairpins into my hand.

I try to stick them into my hair but my burned hand feel clumsy, painful, and they drop to the floor.

Abigail scoops them up and fixes them in my hair. "Your hair's the same color as Miss Lydia's."

"Who?" I ask, not really interested.

"The Brumptons' daughter. She's out walking the beach. Always bringing sand in on her shoes, she is."

A part of me somewhere deep inside wakes up at the mention of a beach.

Abigail pats my shoulder. "Now put your cap on. The afternoon tea won't make itself, you know."

We make the Brumptons' tea with real tea leaves, and this being Sunday, I'm told I'm allowed a break in my room.

Unable to think any more, I climb the stairs to my room and go kneel at the tiny window. As I stare at the view, tears prick my eyes, and the dollhouse shapes of the cottages and sea shimmer and melt into one.

Such a lovely village. So pretty.

I want to go home.

My tears spill down my face and I wipe them away. I watch as a fishing boat floats on the sea in the distance.

Such a quiet house.

My mind drifts, my eyelids grow heavy.

So quiet, so peaceful.

I drift off and dream of that boat lost on the sea.

"Time to go," Abigail calls from behind my door.

Time for another awkward meal with strangers.

Servants' Supper
Legs shaky—sit
Stare at the table scratches
Hands shaky—pass the plates
Too tired to talk
Too tired to think
Just eat

There are dirty plates to be taken to the scullery and water to be boiled for the Brumptons' hot water bottles. It says ten minutes to ten on the grandfather clock when I drag my feet behind Gerty up the stairs in the shadow of her candle. Only the thought of a long hot soak in the tub gets me up the last flight.

Gerty hands me a box of matches for my room, and I go and light my pathetic stub of a candle with one.

I wrap myself in my bathrobe. There's something in the right-hand pocket. It's my movie, still there where I'd placed it a hundred years ago last night.

I'd better hide it.

I open the top dresser drawer. At the back is an envelope with the words Hat Pin written on it in worn-out pencil. Inside, is a long pin with a crystal on the end. I gaze at it for a second. Try to imagine myself pinning a hat on. 1912 style. But I'm falling on my feet, so I tuck the hatpin back inside its envelope and hide the movie under it.

The other drawers are empty.

Holding my candle lamp with one hand, and protecting the flickering flame with the other, I make my way to the bathroom. The bath water flows as cold as Niagara Falls.

I sit on the edge of the tub with my head in my hands.

Now what?

Looking up, I see a water-splashed notice on the wall. I lift my flickering candle to it:

Servants Allowed One Bath a Week.

But it doesn't matter because there's no soap. I can't even have a wash. And just to finish off the hardest, longest day of my life, there's no toothpaste. Someone's left a can of tooth powder on the sink. I taste it. Disgusting. But I brush my teeth with it anyway, using the tip of my finger.

On my way back to my room, my candle dies.

"Who gives a care," I mumble, finally collapsing into bed.

CLOSE ENCOUNTERS OF THE WEIRD KIND

The pounding on the door shatters my sleep.

"Wake up!" someone shouts.

"What?" I call out in the dark. I feel I've been asleep for five minutes.

"I've fetched ya tea."

"Who's that?"

"'Tis Gerty."

"Who?"

"Scullery maid. Gerty."

"But it's still night," I protest.

"Nay mind, time to get up."

"Urrh." Under the bed covers I bend my knees, my stomach muscles tighten and I shiver. Dreading what lies ahead, I grip the bed covers. Cold as it is, why can't I hide in this room, high above the rest of the house? Why do I have to face the day?

But if I don't face the day, I'm never going to find a way back to Gran. I sit up and try to rub some life into my frozen toes. Now I step stiffly across the creaky hardwood floor and open the door, picking up the tea Gerty's left.

It's cold.

I leave it on my dresser and impatiently brush away a tear with the back of my hand. It was a nice thing Gerty did. I should have said thanks. Pulling my robe round my shoulders, thoughts of hot showers and soft soapy baths again flit through my mind. *Gran, Gran, help me.* And I fold over in two.

Someone bangs on my door again. With shaking fingers, I pull my uniform on and stuff my hair under my cap.

Day two on the set of *Brumpton Manor*.

* * *

"Why, but you look half starved, lass," Mrs. Meadowcroft says when she sees me.

"I am a bit hungry," I answer.

"Nay, lass, I mean you look half froze to death. Gets yourself a nice cuppa to warm ya bones."

In the kitchen, the teakettle's boiling, the gaslights are hissing and the cat's lying by the stove. I rush over to the stove and hold my hands out.

"You mustn't be nesh, lass."

I've no idea what Mrs. Meadowcroft is going on about. It's as if these people come from another planet, the way they talk.

A crunching sound makes me look up at the window.

"Gerty, lass!" Mrs. Meadowcroft calls in the direction of the scullery. "Milkman."

I shake my head in disbelief at the scene through the window as Gerty rushes out. The milkman is driving a huge black horse and cart over the driveway. The milkman stops the horse and waves to Gerty. He jumps down and ladles milk from the back of his cart into cans. Gerty must be freezing out there, but she doesn't seem in a hurry to leave.

Mrs. Meadowcroft hands me my tea. "Don't tell the butler I gave you two sugars—he weighs our rations." She sniffs.

I stand next to the stove, taking little sips. It's the best hot drink I've ever tasted.

"Yes, lass, that's the spirit."

I lower myself onto the rocking chair next to the warm stove. The cat leaps into my lap, and I have to steady my cup.

Mrs. Meadowcroft shakes her head. "I've never seen Smudge do that before. He's taken a real shine to you."

Smudge purrs in my lap. "How old is he?"

"Let me think." Mrs. Meadowcroft opens the top of the stove and drops in a lump of coal from the bucket. "We've had him getting nigh on twelve years. I remember 'cos Lydia was about to start school and she were only six. He turned up in the kitchen one day wearing his name, and he's been with us ever since. Eee, but he was such a cuddly kitten back then."

Gerty pushes through the door, carrying the milk.

"Icebox, lass," Mrs. Meadowcroft says to her. She looks at me. "Not that we need ice this time of year."

Mrs. Meadowcroft takes my cup off me. "Gerty," she calls again. "Send breakfast dishes to dining room."

Gerty fills the dumbwaiter with clean plates. As she starts pulling on the rope, Smudge jumps down from my lap to his spot by the stove and watches her.

The dumbwaiter—innocently going up the chute—draws me over to it like a living thing. I'm supposed to be working, making up fires, dusting the morning room. I'm postponing the inevitable, I know, but I can't really be a maid in 1912. Can I?

"Move, girl," Birkett hisses in my ear.

I scream and run through the kitchen.

"Leave the lass alone," I hear Mrs. Meadowcroft say, as I dart into the passageway.

Another day with that man! I don't think I can take it.

I hear his footsteps on the stone floor and dash into the nearest doorway. He walks past without seeing me. I stay frozen to the spot.

The small room I'm in is filled with old lamps and lanterns lined up on a shelf. A pair of legs pass by the window. I lean forward and look up. Adrian's outside, holding a bucket of coal. His brown hair is flattened down and one of his curls has escaped and looks like a question mark. I tap on the window. He sees me, and his face lights up. I wave, and he waves back. I take a deep breath and go collect my cleaning box and cinder pail from the supply cupboard.

"And rolling," I hear the director of my movie say.

* * *

All the coal buckets are filled to overflowing. Lucky. But it takes ages to start the fires. And it feels weird knowing that a Brumpton is lying there asleep. The last bedroom fire I have to light is Lydia's. Trying not to make a sound, I open her door.

The drapes are half closed, but there's enough light now to see that her floor's strewn with dresses, hats, shoes, stockings and underwear. Should I pick them up? Or tiptoe round to get to the fireplace? I glance at the sleeping Lydia and decide to pick them up.

I lift up a corset first. It feels stiff. Who'd want to wear that? I drop it into a drawer in disgust.

Her dresses are surprisingly light. I scoop up a pink one edged in delicate lace. Another has narrow powder blue stripes running through it. They look like prom dresses. I pretend they're costumes.

I open the wardrobe—it creaks—I snap my head round to

check Lydia hasn't moved. She hasn't, so I pull an empty coat hanger off the rail. A fur coat is hanging there. Yuck. I try not to touch it.

Now I pick up the shoes and place them in the wardrobe next to a pair of soft beige lace-up boots. That done, I throw the stockings in with the corset and go scoop up the two hats. One has long feathers poking out the side, and one has a blue ribbon threaded through its wide brim. I've never worn a hat in my life, except for a baseball cap. I place the hat with the ribbon on my head.

"It suits you." Lydia's voice from the bed says, making me jump.

"What's your name?"

I pull the hat off. "Sally Soforth."

"Well, Sally Soforth, as you can see, I was trying on a few clothes for my trip last night."

I like the sound of her voice. It goes up and down like music.

I hold out both hats. "Where d'you want me to put these?"

"Just fling them on the chair. I'll find their boxes later."

I place the hats down on the chair and run my fingernail along one of the feathers. It makes a soft zip sound.

Lydia props herself up in bed with her elbows. I watch her long braids fall over the covers. Abigail was right: her hair *is* the same color as mine.

She shivers, and I glance over at the fireplace.

"I'd better light the fire."

"Oh, yes. Don't let me stop you."

I go kneel down at the fireplace and clean out the grate, disturbing soot and ash and generally making a mess.

Lydia turns on her side and watches me. I try not to notice.

"Where're you from?" she asks. "Not Yorkshire with that accent."

I sweep up the cinders and ashes and drop them into the cinder pail. "The south," I answer vaguely.

"Gracious, mother is casting her net wide these days." She yawns and stretches. "How're you liking it?"

How do I like being away from Gran? Eating meals with strangers? Lighting coal fires on my hands and knees in a freezing house with a bazillion stairs?

"It's different."

"Yes, I suppose it is." Lydia gazes at the clouds out the window. "Oh, well, I should get up." She flops back onto her pillow. "Why bother? All I do lately is try on clothes."

I smear the fireplace grate with black polish. "They're such beautiful clothes, though."

Lydia gazes up at the ceiling. "What use are clothes when my mind's going to rot?" She sits up again. "It's even too cold for tennis." She plucks a book off her nightstand—*Lawn Tennis for Ladies*—and flips through its pages. "Not that Father approves. He says it's unhealthy for females to exert themselves."

That's nice of him, I think, sweat pouring down my face as I polish the grate and stack it with scrunched-up newspaper.

And there it is staring up at me. In bold black newspaper print. Over an ad for Cozy Dozy pajamas.

The year.

1912.

"Are you unwell?" Lydia's very proper English voice reaches me.

No. I'm in 1912. I really am. I didn't want to believe it, but it says so there in black and white.

"I'm fine."

Lydia's watching me, so I light the paper. Not much happens to the fire. I'm doing something wrong but don't know what. I leave it and pick up my cinder pail and cleaning box. "It was very nice to meet you, Miss." Why am I being so polite? Must be Lydia's English accent affecting me. Or the date.

Lydia yawns and stretches again. "Don't let mother wear you out."

I smile and close the door.

My smile dies.

Birkett's staring down at me. I wait for him to speak, but he just keeps on staring.

"I've lit the bedroom fires, Mr. Birkett." I want to shout at him—"It's 1912. It really is."

"I can see that," he says in his quiet but spiteful way. "Your face is filthy."

I touch my face and feel it burning.

"I find it difficult to believe you've even put soap to water this morning. Did you wash in the slop bucket?"

"No," I mumble.

"Get out of my sight."

I take my cleaning box and pail and walk towards the servants' stairs.

"Come back!" Birkett barks.

I drag myself back to face him.

"What has Wainwright given you to do?"

"Who's Wainwright?"

"Abigail, Abigail, Ab-i-gail."

Why didn't he say so in the first place? There's no need to burst a vein.

"Well?" he asks, moving closer. "I'm waiting."

"Nothing, Mr. Birkett." Which is true because I haven't seen her yet.

"Are you deliberately trying to sound like an imbecile?"

I stare at the top of his greasy head. He pokes his face into mine and his stale breath makes me want to gag.

"Look. I can't work with girls who don't show me respect." He jabs his finger at me. "Or girls who don't know what they're doing. Get your things and get out."

The door behind us opens. Lydia appears wearing a light blue robe.

A look of annoyance crosses Birkett's face but quickly changes to a false friendly one. "Sorry to disturb you, Miss." He uses a tone of voice I haven't heard him use before. Polite.

"What's going on?" Lydia asks Birkett but looks at me.

"Nothing to concern yourself with, Miss Lydia," Birkett reassures.

"Then why are you asking Sally here to leave?"

Birkett doesn't miss a beat. "She's not working out, that's all. I'll telephone the agency for her replacement. I'm sorry you had to hear." And he looks sorry too.

Lydia pulls a face. "You know Mother doesn't trust the agency. Since Sally here is new, don't you think we should give her another chance?"

Lydia doesn't wait for his reply. "Well, that's all sorted. Off you go."

Birkett's face is unreadable. "Just as you wish."

Lydia closes her bedroom door.

Without warning, Birkett grabs my arm and wrenches me along the hallway. My cleaning box and cinder pail swing madly about.

At the top of the servants' stairs he pushes a fist into my spine, his other hand squeezes my arm. I'm balanced on the edge; he shakes my arm and a lump of cinder falls from my pail and bounces down each step—bump, bump, bump.

"I'm watching you," he whispers, and a drop of his wet spit lands in my ear.

He gives me another shake and pinches my arm with his sharp nails. "Now get."

I start down the stairs. I want to run and run and run.

"And straighten your cap," I hear him hiss above me.

I don't look back.

ESCAPE

What just happened? The man's mad. I race to the kitchen. The kitchen feels safe. Mrs. Meadowcroft feels safe. I stand close to her table, watching her mix pastry in a brown bowl, trying to find any excuse to stay.

"Now, lass, how are you?" she asks, pouring sugar from a pan off the old-fashioned metal weighing scales into her bowl.

I fight back my tears. I want to tell her about Birkett but don't know if I should. I remember I'm supposed to be acting. I check for a camera.

"I'm good." I turn and stare at the dumbwaiter. Right. It didn't work yesterday. I'll go there tonight when the house is asleep.

One of the bells ring, and the sound shakes my nerves.

Mrs. Meadowcroft drops her pastry dough onto the kitchen table and pats it into a ball. "That'll be Mrs. Brumpton. She wants to see you in the morning room."

"Why?"

Perhaps Birkett's been talking; discussing me. I rub my arm in the place his pointy nails pinched my skin.

Playing for time, I take a round weight off the end of the scales and make the scales seesaw. What if Mrs. Brumpton realizes I shouldn't be working for her? What if she sees I'm acting?

Mrs. Meadowcroft cuts her pastry into a flower shape. "Go on," she says, losing patience. She wipes her hands on her apron, leans over and straightens my cap. "And don't forget to call her ma'am."

Out in the cold passageway, I spy Birkett closing his office door and my stomach twists into a knot.

"Stop running," he snarls, as I race past.

I slow down but can sense his eyes burning into my back. I take the stone steps up to the Brumptons' part of the house and don't look up until I almost bang into the front door. Staring at the door, I wonder whether to make a run for it. But to where? And how would I survive? Shouldn't I stay close to the dumbwaiter? My ticket home. The sun shines through the door's green and red stained glass. I lift my head and bathe in the warmth on my face. It'd be so easy to open this door and escape.

This house.

This job.

Birkett.

My hand hovers over the handle. Somewhere in the distance a train whistle blows.

"Sally."

I turn and see Adrian bouncing down the Brumptons' curving staircase. He stops and smiles and our eyes lock. You're one of us—the look in his eyes says—you're a friend. And his smile warms me more than the sun at the door.

"Where're you going?" he asks when he reaches me.

"To meet with Mrs. Brumpton."

"Not to worry, then. She'll like you."

* * *

"Act four: Scene one," I whisper, struggling to stay calm in the moment. "Act four: Scene one."

Mrs. Brumpton sweeps into the morning room, filling the air with the scent of flowers. Two little brown dogs, limping behind her black skirt, are trying to keep up.

"Good morning," she says in a breathless voice. She nods at me, smiling. Her hair's swept up into a loose round bun. She takes a seat on a high-back chair close to the glowing fire, and tilts her head to one side.

I have this weird feeling I've seen her before.

"Now," she begins. "I know Birkett hired you."

So—she thinks Birkett hired me, and he thinks she did—neat.

"But we can still have our little talk, can't we...Sally?"

She doesn't wait for my answer.

"Is everyone treating you properly?"

You mean apart from Birkett trying to throw me down the stairs?

"Yes, thank you ... ma'am." And I feel like a checkout lady, saying ma'am.

"Splendid. You see, I expect this house to be kept spotless. I call it my war-on-dirt." She pauses to make her point. "Your new uniform has arrived so you can give back the one you're wearing." She lowers her voice as if telling me a secret. "I've included some undergarments."

Thoughtful. If she means underwear.

"The cost is—let me see"—she looks down at a piece of paper on a foldout tea table: "two pounds, four shillings and nine pence. That sum will be deducted from your wages at two shillings a week."

Not so thoughtful, then.

"Your wages are five shillings a week, paid quarterly. Do you understand?"

Quarterly? What if I'm stuck here for more than a few days? I'll need bathroom stuff, at least.

I try out my new acting skills and ask, "Can't I be paid weekly, ma'am? I don't have any money."

Mrs. Brumpton gives me a long look. "What do you need money for?"

I think she's joking, so I start to smile.

Her expression stays deadly serious.

I remember what Abigail told me about the last maid. How her mom took all her pay. "To send money home," I lie, and I wish it were true.

"Very well. I'll instruct Birkett to pay you weekly."

"Thanks." Oops! I forgot to add the ma'am, but I'm too embarrassed now to say it.

She gives me a slow sideways nod. "You'll get one Sunday off a month as well as one day and one evening per week. Now, Sally, most maids only get one afternoon off a week, so you're very lucky."

I've a strong sensation all this is happening to someone else. It can't be me standing here in a maid's uniform, wearing ankle boots too small for me, listening to this woman wearing too much perfume. Can it? And why doesn't she offer me a seat? The backs of my legs feel like they're being stretched by an elastic band.

One of her dogs, lying curled up in front of the fire, yawns. The other dog places a furry paw on Mrs. Brumpton's shoe. She notices me looking at them. "This is Sniff and Snaff. My very old and very loyal dogs."

"They're cool."

Mrs. Brumpton looks confused. "No. I think they're quite warm here in front of the fire."

"N-No," I stammer, realizing my mistake. "I mean, they're warm...that is...they look comfortable."

"You may go now." Mrs. Brumpton hands me my new uniform wrapped in a string-tied brown paper package.

"And if you have any questions, you can always ask the butler."

Ask that man for advice? Never. But I don't say this out loud. "Thank you, ma'am," I say instead.

And as I head for the door, I glimpse Mrs. Brumpton feeling Sniff and Snaff to see if they are, for sure, warm enough.

ADRIAN

After changing into my new uniform in my room, I return downstairs to find the gaslights have been lowered and the kitchen is deserted. But Adrian's in the servants' dining room, sitting at the scratched table, his book lying open in front of him. The table's lined with newspaper and stacked high with silver—teapots, trays, vases, candlesticks—and other things I don't have the names for.

"Can I sit here?" I ask him.

His gray eyes twinkle. "The maids never usually help me," he says, closing his book.

Not what I meant, but I guess it's better to look busy in case Birkett shows up.

Smudge is under the table and moves onto my boots. Trying not to disturb him, I scratch at my itchy legs. Whoever invented these wool stockings Mrs. Brumpton gave me, never had to wear them.

"Where's Abigail?"

"Didn't she tell you? Afternoon off."

"No, but I've been upstairs. Where's, you-know-who?"

"Doing the books. All day," he adds with a knowing look.

I let myself relax and watch Adrian as he concentrates on

polishing a candlestick. His eyelashes sweep the top of his cheeks, I notice.

"Havin' a grand time?" he asks, placing the now shining candlestick to one side.

"Define grand time."

"Sorry?"

"I'm OK."

"O-what?"

"OK. Fine."

"Grand." He polishes a soup spoon for a few seconds.

"No. I'm not fine."

"You'll get used to it."

"That's what you think," I mumble.

"What?"

"Nothing."

He pauses and his gray eyes look into mine. "You don't have to help me," he says. "You can tell me about your home down south, if you likes."

"I'll help."

He brings me a green apron to protect my white one, and some cotton gloves to protect my hands, and we sit opposite each other, polishing.

"How'd you get on with Mrs. Brumpton? he asks. Give you her war-on-dirt speech, did she?"

"Yeah." I dip my rag into the polish. "She said I have to pay for my uniform."

"Aye. Maids have to."

"Don't you?"

"She hasn't asked in the three years I've worked here."

"What?" I say, looking up from the table. "That's not right."

"But she's generous with your time off."

I don't get his logic but let the matter drop. I won't be paying for my uniform because I won't be here.

"What book are you reading?" I select some tweezer-type gadgets and examine them curiously.

Adrian shows me the front cover. "Peter and Wendy."

I hold the silver tweezers up. Maybe they're for picking up cubes of cheese.

"D'you think," he asks, "it'd make a good moving picture?"

"Um?" I twist the tweezers round and they glint in the gaslight.

"I mean, how'd they film Peter Pan flying? Suppose they could add ropes to him or summat."

"They'll use green-screen technology," I say without thinking, "and you won't see any ropes." I put the tweezers down. "Though the Disney one's drawn by animators without the use of green screens or computers."

Adrian stops in mid-polish and stares at me. A stare that asks *what foreign language are you speaking?* And I realize what I've said must sound crazy to his 1912 ears.

I focus on the newspaper lining the table. "Just something I read about the movies, I mean, moving pictures." I start polishing again and hope he changes the subject.

"Pass me those sugar tongs," he says. "They're done."

So that's what they're for. Picking up sugar cubes. I was nearly right.

We carry on cleaning. We take dull things and make them shine. There's something satisfying about it. We don't really notice that we're working, and we don't really notice that we're talking.

Now he takes his pocket watch out and gives it a quick polish. It shines like a small sun.

"I've never seen a watch like that." I think of something. "Does it tell the date?"

"No. But that's a good idea."

I try something else. It's as if I need to confirm the year

I'm in every few hours. "What year were you born?"

"1897."

"Eighteen, you said! 1897." I can't imagine it.

"I was born May 16th, 1897. I'm nearly fifteen. When were you born?"

"Two thou—, I mean, 19—, I mean, let me see your watch, can I?"

He unthreads the chain and passes it over.

"It were me da's."

"Your what?"

"Me da's. Me father's. He saved the mayor of Whitby when his boat got into trouble and they presented it to him."

Cupping the watch in my left hand, I rub my thumb over its smooth golden surface. It feels warm and heavy and pulses as it ticks.

Adrian leans forward. "Open it, if you like."

I open the lid and gasp.

Engraved on the face is a tall sailing ship floating along a winding river. The sails seem to move, and the water meanders far off into the distance, pulling me along with it. I sense Adrian watching, so I close the lid. It makes a satisfying click sound. "It's from Switzerland," he whispers, as I hand it back.

"You must treasure it."

Adrian looks proud enough to burst. "I'd never let it go."

I swallow the sharp lump in my throat. All I have from my dad is his special edition of *It's a Wonderful Life*.

"Your dad's a boater, then?" I ask, glancing at the stacks of shiny silver things that now outnumber the dull ones.

Adrian picks out a sugar bowl. "He were a fisherman, same as rest o' men in Bay."

"Were? I mean, was?"

He stops polishing. "Aye. He passed four years back."

I stop polishing too. "How?"

"Drowned."

I can barely hear him. "Drowned, you said?"

"Storm of '08."

"You have your mom, then?"

He drops his eyes. "Me ma followed a month after."

I catch my breath. "Why?"

"Bad lungs."

"Oh." I bite my lower lip, trying to think of something better to say than just, oh. I can't, which is weird when you think I've lost my parents too. "Have you always lived in Robin Hood's Bay?" I ask, settling for trying to take that hurt look off his face.

"Aye. Always will."

"Always? That's a long time."

"Best place in Yorkshire and Yorkshire's best place in world."

"Pop quiz—"

"Pop quiz. What's that?"

"It's a test they throw at us at school, and it's . . ." I'm about to say a catchphrase in *Speed,* but stop myself. If this really is 1912, I know Adrian has never heard a word spoken in a movie yet, and I don't want to freak him out after my green-screen comment. "It's the way I start a question. So, pop quiz, why aren't you in school?"

Wow! Now I sound like some sort of annoying public service announcement.

"Why?" Adrian says, frowning. "Same reason as you, suppose."

Oops, he thinks I'm a school dropout.

He snatches up the last fork and starts cleaning it, making his curls bounce. "I'm glad we can leave at twelve. I hated school. They said I were stupid."

"Nice." No school after age twelve. Crazy.

"Just 'cos I got me d's and b's twisted round."

"That'll mess with your head."

He stops polishing. "I like that—mess with your head."

He looks at me as if I've just invented physiology 101 or something. I try not to feel flattered.

"Anyroad," Adrian adds. "I needed to bring some brass in."

"Brass?"

"Money. Don't you speak any English?"

I pretend he's joking. "Would you go back to school? If you got the chance."

"When they beat the livin' daylights out of you for not writing proper? Dump you in bottom row when you *know'd* you'd done your best work ever?"

"Sounds terrible." I think of my own school for a moment. How I hate it when teachers say those dreaded, panic-stirring words: Get in pairs.

"I do take the donkey path to school gates sometimes," Adrian says, making me look up.

"Oh, why's that?"

He puts down the last silver fork and shuts the polish lid. "To get that last-day feeling, all over again."

DAY OFF

The sun's shining, it's my first day off, and I'm going to tell Adrian—my secret.

But not in the house.

No.

In the village.

And now it strikes me. I've been here one whole week and I haven't set foot outside. I can't count reaching behind the kitchen door to drop leftovers in the slop bucket. There's a sign there, actually dug into the wall, which says: SHUT THE DOOR. No please or thank you or would you mind.

Nice.

Anyway, sign or no sign, my stomach's doing handstands at the thought of going out. Last night, it took me ages to get to sleep, plus my poor throbbing feet keep waking me up; and every time I closed my eyes I saw coal buckets. Dancing coal buckets. Up the stairs they went, spilling coal like some sick scene out of *Fantasia*.

Adrian has the day off too, and plans on joining me on the beach near the Lifeboat House after first finishing some chores Birkett's suddenly found for him to do.

I skip breakfast. I'm too wound-up to eat, and I want to make the most of every single minute.

Abigail hands me a cardigan in the kitchen. For protection from the nippy Yorkshire air, she tells me. I thank her, then grumble that Birkett seems to be keeping Adrian busy on purpose.

But once at the scullery door, I forget about Birkett, and even Adrian for the moment, when I realize I'll be leaving the safety of the house and—scary thought—the dumbwaiter.

I lift up the latch. Four scullery steps to climb and I'm outside, actually walking away from the house, and I can't stop gulping the air.

Now I'm on the edge of the winding backyard path. Twice I look back, just to make sure the house hasn't magically disappeared.

But I can't wait to explore the village I can see from my attic window. And I can't wait to see Adrian. Every day, I've wanted to tell him about who I really am. I think I'll burst if I don't.

I pass the stables and the empty vegetable patches, and I reach the back gate. Without looking back this time, I open it, setting off along the trail that I've heard Adrian and the others call the donkey path.

The salty air from the ocean bites, and I'm glad I have Abigail's cardigan. I'm also glad she didn't say anything about me wearing my uniform on my day off. I've left my apron and cap off, but I still think I look like a maid.

In one pocket is my *Groundhog Day* disk, ready to show Adrian, as well as my shopping list for Ma Thompson's, a general store Mrs. Meadowcroft has recommended for much needed supplies. In the other pocket, I have my week's pay. Exactly three shiny shillings. "Your wages, girl, minus uniform deduction," Birkett said last night, and he'd acted reluctant to pass it over as if it were his own money.

I hold the heavy coins in my pocket. Payday feels good. I've no clue what I want to do when I leave school, but when I get back to Orlando, I'll look for a way to help Gran.

Babysitting, yard work. Huh, anything'd be a snap compared with being a maid in a house with a dumbwaiter that won't take me home.

But no.

I won't think about work, or my nightly visits to the dumbwaiter. Today I'm free. Free to explore the village.

THE VILLAGE

Up and down the sun-trapped lanes and sloping steps the camera follows me, while I enjoy the sound made by my boots as they strike the cobblestones and the feel of my long dress brushing against my ankles.

The cottages are so jumbled up, I can't tell where one begins and another one ends. Robin Hood's Bay is like a miniature village that doesn't feel real.

I don't feel real.

Storekeepers, in stiff white aprons, are opening up their shutters and sweeping their steps. I have to jump out of the way just as one of them dumps out a bucket of water. "Sorry, lass," he shouts.

Ma Thompson's (the faded store sign just says Thompsons) has a water pump outside that someone's painted a bright shade of Christmas red. I pump the handle and take a big gulp of cool refreshing water.

Ah, that's better.

A tinkly bell rings when I push open the green-painted door and Ma Thompson gives me a toothless smile. I buy a toothbrush from her.

And a hairbrush. Then ask for shampoo. It hasn't been invented yet. Abigail was right then, when she'd given me vinegar water to rinse with after I'd washed my hair with ordinary, everyday soap. I just hadn't believed her.

I also buy two Cadbury chocolate bars. I've missed chocolate so much, even my dreams of hot showers have changed to dreams of chocolate fountains.

Next, I buy some spare candles for my room. When I'd asked Birkett for a candle, he'd cut one in half and handed it to me as if it were the last copy of the Declaration of Independence or something. Well, now I'll have my own.

I hand Ma Thompson my shillings, hoping she'll take what she needs the way I've seen some foreign tourists do in Orlando.

Ma Thompson takes my coins but wants to know where my accent's from. I tell her I'm from the south, giving her my stock answer to explain away my American accent. It's worked so far. The servants think it means the south of England. But Ma Thompson wants to know more.

Where's Adrian when I need him?

* * *

I go to the steps near the Lifeboat House and scan the beach below. Adrian's nowhere in sight.

So much for his day off.

The tide's out but the steps are still wet, so I gather up the skirt of my dress and climb carefully down to the sand below.

I gaze back along the cliff where the cottages cling to the edge. There's still no sign of Adrian. Maybe he won't come. Maybe he doesn't want to come. What if he's just a work friend and not an all-the-time friend?

I watch as a crab climbs sideways out of a rock pool onto the top of a jutting rock. He stares at me for a second, then scuttles back underneath. It's all right for him, hiding all day, waiting for the tide to bring him his dinner. He doesn't have to deal with difficult store ladies. Or, I think, my stomach churning over, tell his new friend the most incredible story in the history of incredible stories.

I can't do it; I'm going back to the house.

"Hello-o there!" Adrian calls from the top of the steps. He's wearing a cap, and he takes it off and waves at me with it. I wave back.

He sprints down the steps and jumps over the rock pools. As usual, a book is sticking out of his pocket. He looks different in his street clothes: suit pants, too short in the leg, and a sweater, patched at the elbow. I'm beginning to realize there's no such thing as casual clothes in 1912. And no one seems to wear any color. In Robin Hood's Bay, anyway. Black and gray. Black and white. It's not difficult for me to imagine my old movie today.

Adrian reaches me and checks the time on his pocket watch. "Nearly ten. 'Tis supposed to be me day off. Birkett must've got wind I wanted to leave early."

"You're here now. Forget Birkett."

We find a flat rock to sit on, and we listen to the rise and fall of the gentle waves.

I look at the sea, at the village, up at the cliffs—anything to take my mind off the subject of time travel. I point to the cliffs. "Why did they build those cottages so close to the edge?"

"They didn't. The edge got closer." He points behind him. "See up there?"

"Yeah."

"That used to be the top of King Street till it tumbled in a storm. But you said you wanted to tell me something."

I hesitate.

"Go on. You can tell me owt. I won't think you're gormless."

"Gormless?"

"Aye, gormless, stupid. Birkett's not been upsetting you again, has he?"

"No more than usual."

For once, I can't discuss Birkett. The tide is coming in, so I nod towards the top of the cliff. "Let's go up there." Maybe walking and talking at the same time will help.

At the steps, Adrian reaches for my arm.

"I can manage," I tell him, my nerves making me sound harsh.

"Well, mind you don't slip," he warns, as if I were a breakable doll and not a girl who climbs stairs all day.

We pass a sign directing us to Boggle Hole and Ravenscar one way, Whitby the other, and as we follow the cliff path in the direction of Boggle Hole, my stomach takes a tumble.

"I'm not from here," I blurt out.

"Aye, I know."

"No. You don't."

"Oh?"

"I'm from across the pond."

"What? Boggle Hole pond?"

I stop walking. Adrian turns and looks at me. His gray eyes, the same color as the sea below, have such an innocent expression.

"No. Not Boggle Hole pond."

"Down south, right?"

"Yes. But not the south you think. Further. Far across the ocean." And I stare at the ocean and try to imagine America out there on the horizon.

I take a deep breath of sea air and tell him...

Everything.

I talk for a long time, trying to explain the things I don't understand myself.

Silence.

"Do you believe me?"

He kicks at the sandy soil under his feet. The sea breeze makes me shiver. Of course he doesn't believe me. Would I believe me, if I were him?

THE FUTURE OR THE PAST?

"Say something, you're making me nervous."

"Let me think." Adrian pulls away.

"I've this from the future, if it'll help." I take my *Groundhog Day* movie from my pocket and hand it to him.

He turns the little disk over. If only I could show him how it works. The disk on its own doesn't prove a thing. Though it does look futuristic compared with Mr. Brumpton's huge gramophone records.

Adrian smiles. He does believe me. A wave of relief pours through my body.

"I think the job's got to you," he says, and I collapse inside. "It's not your fault. You're from the south where they're soft, mollycoddled and . . . and now you're all done-in."

He doesn't believe me.

I start to run.

He catches up as I fall to the ground. I've no fight left. I'm all alone, the truth tied only to me, weighing me down.

"Don't run off like that!"

His angry words make me sit up.

"You think I've lost my mind."

"I never said that. You're tired, that's all."

What's the use? I slump back down.

"Don't take on, I believe you," he says, but I don't believe him.

He pulls me up. "I always thought you were strange. Showing up without bags or belongings."

And now he says something I know I'll never, ever forget.

"Dumbwaiter or no dumbwaiter, you and me are friends for life."

QUESTIONS

Feeling the need to run again, I race towards the village.

"Hold your horses," Adrian calls after me. "Look—a magpie." He reaches out and points to a big black-and-white bird pecking at the ground. I'm about to run on, but he holds up his hand. "Not yet," he says. "Look for another."

"Why?"

"One for sorrow, two for joy."

We both search the meadows with our eyes.

"There's one," I point out.

"Good," he says. "Two for joy."

And he smiles.

* * *

In a little tea shop on Chapel Street, we order a pot of hot chocolate and two toasted raisin buns. Adrian makes the mistake of telling the waitress he doesn't like tea, and she goes into a two-minute speech on all the reasons he should.

When she's gone, Adrian stares at me with a funny look.

"What?" I ask, when his staring lasts too long.

"Pop puzzle: What's it like in your time?" he asks, forgetting the phrase should be pop quiz.

QUESTIONS

I take it as a good sign he's curious. But before I can tell him, the waitress returns and places our order on the table in our cozy corner by the window. "Two toasted teacakes and cocoa." She glances at the skirt of my dress. "Servant girl," she says under her breath.

"Pardon?" Adrian asks.

She smiles at him sweetly. "Nothing."

Hey, I don't see much difference between her and me. She serves people too, doesn't she?

"So," Adrian says when she's gone. "The future?"

Warming my hands on my cup, I try to explain. "There are cars—"

"Motorcars?"

"Yes. And buses."

"Omnibuses?"

"Umm. Yes. I think so."

"Are there trams?"

"I don't know. Shut up. Everyone owns a vehicle."

"In America?"

"Yes."

I rattle on, answering all his questions. To my ears, I sound like a teacher, but Adrian says he likes listening to my voice. My American voice.

"What's your town like?" he asks.

"Well, Dad used to say Orlando's the town the mouse built."

I explain about Mickey Mouse, then try to describe theme parks. As much as I've discovered from the Monday-morning conversations I've overheard at school. "They're these magical worlds with rides that spin you around or dip you into water."

"Do you like painting?" Adrian asks.

I frown. "Don't think so. Why?"

"You've painted a nice picture in me head."

I place my cup down. "Forget it. Let's go."

"Nay. I didn't mean owt. Tell me which rides you like best."

"Never been. Everyone thinks I'm stuck-up because I won't meet up at Cinderella Castle." I take a sip of hot chocolate. "Huh. Better to be thought stuck-up than hard-up."

"Tell me about your gran, then."

I feel my throat closing and have to cough. "Gran goes to Bingo every week, trying to win me theme-park tickets."

"Does she win?"

"Gran never loses at Bingo. She 'nearly wins.'"

Adrian thinks Gran sounds nice. I tell him about how she hoards stuff. And about Aunt Dottie. How she even keeps ruined photographs of girls with their faces all blurred.

Adrian doesn't laugh. "That's all they've got: their memories." He pulls out his golden pocket watch. "So they'll never throw them out, will they?"

"Haven't you two got homes to go to?" the waitress wants to know.

Adrian insists on paying. "Girls shouldn't pay when there's a boy around."

"That's dumb," I tell him.

He raises his eyebrows.

I tell him about my trouble at Ma Thompson's with the money.

He spreads his coins out on the white tablecloth. "This is a penny—twelve pennies in a shilling. A shilling—twenty shillings in a pound. Here's a farthing—a quarter penny. Oh, and this big coin is half-a-crown—two shillings and sixpence."

"What's this one?" I ask, picking up an unusual heart-shaped coin.

"That's me lucky penny I found on the donkey path first day of work. I always keeps it in me pocket—not that I'm superstitious, mind—but I'd feel funny without it."

* * *

Outside, Adrian bugs me to tell him some more about the future. I talk about televisions, computers, the web. By the time we reach the donkey path I'm onto cell phones.

"Pop quiz," Adrian says, getting it right this time. "What about wires?"

"No wires. People even ride skateboards on the phone."

"What's a skateboard?"

I explain, then demonstrate by gliding along on an imaginary skateboard on the donkey path.

"Yes, moving machines. C'mon, Sally. Think like a boy."

I pretend to fall off my skateboard. "You mean act like I don't have any brains?"

He stuffs his hands in his pockets. "Don't you think I've got brains, then?"

I resist the temptation to start singing If I Only Had a Brain. I've noticed before, Adrian doesn't understand sarcasm.

"Just kiddin'. You want action stuff, right? How about flying?" I look up to the sky. Nothing but birds. And nothing like Orlando.

I start wondering about Gran's flight home. Has she gone? Or is she still at Aunt Dottie's waiting for me? She hates being out of her routine. She hates other people's coffee. I turn to the sea and try to send a message across it. *I'm OK, Gran. Don't worry, I'll get home soon.*

"What about flying?" Adrian asks, bringing me back.

"People get on planes as if they're just catching a"—I'm about to say bus, but Robin Hood's Bay doesn't have a bus service yet—"train," I finish, remembering the sound of the train whistle I heard at the house.

He gazes up at the sky. "But wouldn't all those flying machines crash into each other?"

I have to go into long explanations about air traffic controllers and radios. This leads to space travel. Adrian wants to know everything, and I'm beginning to feel like a walking Wikipedia. "Now enough with the questions. What are you, five?"

"It'd be grand to live in your world."

I try to ignore the fact he didn't say your time. Does he think I'm imagining everything, after all?

We reach the house, and I open the gate. Smudge is there, as if waiting for us. I bend down and stroke his warm fur. "Let's get him some milk." And I smile to myself, thinking about the milkman and Gerty, and Mrs. Meadowcroft saying yesterday the milk will go sour while we wait for her to bring it in.

"What're you smiling about?" Adrian asks as we pass the stables.

"Oh, just about the fridge," I answer, going one last time into teacher mode. "It's like the icebox except it runs off electricity. You open the door, a light turns on, you take out your food. Easy."

"Does the light go out when you close the door?"

"Course."

"How d'you know the light goes out, if thee can't see it?"

"Ah," I tell him, "that's one of life's great mysteries."

HARD-KNOCK LIFE

A bell rings, and Adrian jumps up from the scratched table.

"Hold on there, boy," Birkett snaps. "I have a list for the village."

Adrian taps my chair as he passes. I try to hide my happiness from Birkett.

Birkett doesn't notice. He's busy reading Adrian's list. "And you can go to Scarborough on the train for Mr. Brumpton's cigars."

Hmm. I wonder if I can sneak out with him. I've never been on a train before. Or to Scarborough.

"Oh, Gerty, there you are," Mrs. Meadowcroft says. "Sally'll help you with the wash."

What!

Gerty flops down on her chair and gives me a grateful look, then swiftly drops her eyes and studies the scratches on the table.

"Young Sally." Mrs. Meadowcroft stirs her tea. "You can do the scrubbing and rinsing. And where's your cap?"

"I forgot it."

"Nay mind, I think there's a spare one in the cupboard."

Adrian looks up and smiles at me. He knows I can't stand my cap. Birkett eyes me as if he's going to make a comment.

He settles for a sneer. Talking about the laundry is probably way beneath him. Where's Abigail? I wonder. She's the one who normally gives me my Monday morning duties.

Adrian beats me to it.

"Where's Abigail, Mrs. Meadowcroft?" he asks.

"She's with Mrs. Brumpton," Mrs. Meadowcroft answers. "They've gone to get tickets."

Tickets for what, I wonder.

But Birkett stands up. "Breakfast is over. Get on with your duties."

"Breakfast is over," Adrian mimics, mouthing the words and facing me so Birkett can't see. "Get on with your duties."

I smother a giggle; his impersonation of Birkett is dead on.

Birkett glares at me. "Do you have anything important to share with the rest of us, girl?"

"No, Mr. Birkett."

"Then do us all a favor and shut up."

Rushing to get away—who needs a cap—I follow Gerty into the wash-house but stop when I see the stacks of soiled laundry piled on the floor.

"Where do we start?" I ask, wishing for once I was upstairs doing my own job.

"With the whites," Gerty answers, lifting a dirty cotton hanky.

"Yuck. Did I ever tell you about Kleenex?"

Gerty gives me a blank look.

"Forget it."

She pours Persil washing powder into a massive round tub filled with steaming hot water. Then pounds the washing with something that looks like a four-legged stool at the end of a broomstick.

Just my luck to go time travelling before washing machines.

But there's no time to dream. Gerty's hauling the first

sheet out and she wants me to rinse it. After, she gets me to haul the rinsed sheet into a big round tub.

The tub's full now, and we both bump it up the washhouse steps, dragging it into the brick-walled yard where the freezing air stings our raw hands. Without a cap, strands of my hair fall onto my face. I push them behind my ears.

I can't believe Gerty does this every week on her own. And I realize, guiltily, that all I know about her is she's sixteen. I watch her as she uncovers a metal stand with huge wooden rollers. It has nasty metal cogs on one side and a big handle on the other.

"Would you mind," she asks, "turning yon mangle."

Gerty feeds a dripping sheet into its rollers. I turn the handle in a wide circle and the rollers squeeze the water from the sheet.

"Adrian's lucky," I mumble. "Catching the train."

"Aye. But he could do with the rest."

I look at Gerty. "What d'you mean? His job's much easier than ours."

"Don't you know? He gets up before dawn to bring up ye coal. Not just from coal shed to back door. Nay. He lugs it all the way to yon bedrooms." She pauses to feed in a sheet. "He's even stacked kindling wood in your pail 'cos he knows thee forget."

I stop winding.

"You must be right chuffed."

"Chuffed?"

"I thought you'd be."

Wow. So Adrian's been helping me. I smile. He's a real friend. I start winding the roller again. I just wish I knew for sure he believed my story.

Gerty looks down at the laundry. "I wish I had an Adrian. There's thirteen of us at home but that's not the same: brothers and sisters."

Thirteen! Talk about *Cheaper by the Dozen*.

She reaches over and pushes me. "Here, watch your hair."

I take a step back from the rollers. "There's got to be a better way to earn a dollar . . . I mean, a pound."

Her soft brown eyes stare up at me. "It's not so bad. I'm as strong as a cart-'orse." She watches me struggle to turn the mangle's handle. "Let us do that."

We swap positions with me guiding sheets into the rollers. Then I help her hang the sheets on a washing line. After some time has passed, I notice the first sheet at the end of the line looks weird, stiff—frozen! I snap it with my fingers. We move back to work the mangle, and I can't stop thinking about the frozen sheet. Will it be able to dry like that? Or will we have to haul it back to the wash-house? I mean, are we wasting our time out here?

"Your hair!" Gerty shouts. "Your beautiful hair!"

Too late. A great clump of my hair has twisted round a roller. I tug at my scalp.

"Get it off! Get it off!" I shout, trying to stand perfectly still, while bent in two.

Gerty unwinds the roller and pulls my hair through, strand-by-painful-strand. I touch my sore scalp. She brings her hand down and catches the nasty metal cogs on the side of the mangle.

"You're bleeding!" I shout.

She lifts her hand to her mouth.

"Let me see."

"Nay mind that," Gerty says, "How's your head?"

I touch my sore scalp. "I'll live." But Gerty's hand is oozing red blood. "Let me get you a Band-Aid."

"What's one of those when 'tis at home?"

Before I can explain, Birkett shows up in the yard. "What's going on here?" He glares at me. "Work, girl."

I snatch up a sheet.

"Work faster, girl, faster," he orders.

"I'm trying, Mr. Birkett." I fight the dripping sheet. The sheet fights back.

"I find that difficult to believe."

Why does he always say that? As if he thinks everyone's always lying to him. With a huge effort, I push down the anger his words stir up.

"No, faster. If you want to be in service, you'll have to work faster." Birkett narrows his eyes at Gerty. "Why aren't you working?"

"She's cut herself," I jump in. "You'd better let her go fix it."

Birkett's face goes purple. "GET OUT OF MY SIGHT!" he shouts at me. "Do you hear me? GET!" Mr. Quiet has gone missing and been replaced with this shouting nut.

I stand frozen to the spot. Gerty looks frozen too.

Birkett clenches both fists and shakes them at her. "You stupid . . . you'd better not get blood on those sheets." He takes a step forward. "Don't just stand there, girl."

Gerty drops her arms into the tub. Her bloodied hand brushes a wet sheet. A red stain grows across the whiteness like a crawling insect.

Birkett walks so fast towards her that his last step kicks her leg. She stumbles sideways. I can't swear he did it on purpose, but then again, I can't swear he didn't. But when he lifts his hand up, I shield her, finding my voice at last.

"You can't do that. It's against the law."

Birkett pushes his face into mine, so close, I can count the veins on his nose.

"Law? Law? What law? The only law in this house is my law." And he turns on his squeaky-clean shoes, and leaves.

"I hate him," I hiss under my breath. "I hate him."

Gerty gathers up the stained sheet. "I can wash it off see, I can wash it off," she says over and over.

I place my hand on her shoulder. "Leave it—no—leave it. Go fix your hand; I'll do this."

Gerty struggles up.

I put my arm around her.

"Let's go tell Mrs. Meadowcroft."

She pulls away. "'Twas my fault."

"Your fault!"

Gerty pulls away and slouches towards the wash-house steps, the stained sheet draped over her arms.

"Gerty," I call, but she doesn't answer. I run after her.

"If I tell Mrs. Meadowcroft," she says to shut me up. "She'll tell Mrs. Brumpton, and they'll replace me, not him."

"Why?"

"A man's job comes first."

I want to argue, but there's panic in her eyes. I have to give in.

She makes a rough bandage for her hand, and we go back to work, both too tired and too miserable to talk. Scrub, soak, pound, rinse and wring, hang on the line. Again and again, all day long, until my head's pounding and my body feels wrung out.

At last we go in for our meal. Adrian's not there. He's still in Scarborough. There's no one to turn to. And nothing I can do.

Gerty won't let me.

TRAPPED

Mrs. Meadowcroft lifts a thick-crusted apple pie out the oven, filling the kitchen with delicious baking smells.

One of the bells on the wall rings. "Now," she says to me. "I want you to go to the dining room and side the pots."

"Do what with the pots?"

She lifts her head to the ceiling. "Oh for a Yorkshire lass who can understand me—clear the dishes away, clear the dishes."

She takes a bowl of cream and thickens it into snow peaks with a whisk. "Just stack the dinner plates in the dumbwaiter and send them to the kitchen."

I stare at the dumbwaiter. It looks so normal. So solid. Did I dream my passage down?

"D'you hear me, lass? Why are you always staring at the wall?"

I pull my eyes from the dumbwaiter. "You want me to stack the plates."

"Yes," she says. "And for heaven's sake, straighten your cap."

* * *

It's quiet in the dining room. Library quiet. The gaslights are turned high and the red velvet drapes are closed against the night. I scan the room for Birkett.

Good. He's not here.

But Adrian is.

Keeping my head down, I tiptoe over to the dumbwaiter and watch him at work. He gives me a friendly nod as he fills Lydia's bowl with creamy soup. This is the first time I've seen the family sitting all together. Yet they all look strangely familiar. Are they my relations? Gran and Aunt Dottie never mentioned any Brumptons. But maybe Gran did, and I never listened. I watch them closely.

Mr. Brumpton is at one end of the table, reading a magazine with antique cars on the cover—wrong, it's 1912, so they must be new. Sniff and Snaff are under the table at Mrs. Brumpton's buttoned shoes. Lydia's close to her mother, sitting ballerina straight in a silky dress, her auburn hair swept loosely up and dotted with sparkly crystals.

They all look like a movie still.

But Lydia turns to her mother, and the picture is broken. "Mother, I am a decoration," she says.

Mrs. Brumpton looks up. "Yes, dear, you look lovely tonight. Did Abigail do your hair? And those earrings are extremely pretty against your dress."

Lydia blinks. "Not how I look; how I live. I want some meaning to my life."

"You will. Soon you'll meet a nice young man and get married."

"I'm never getting married."

Mrs. Brumpton picks up her soup spoon. "Every girl dreams of a husband and a home of her own."

"Surely there's more to life than just being someone's wife?"

"You'll feel differently when you meet the right person. Now finish your soup, dear, before it gets cold."

But Lydia doesn't touch her soup. "Father, what if I get a profession? Do something useful with my time."

Mr. Brumpton glances up from his car magazine. "What's that, you say? What do you want?"

"I was saying—if you'll pay attention—I might learn a profession."

"No daughter of mine needs to work," he says, sounding insulted at the suggestion.

"But," Lydia begins.

"But nothing. I own a gas lamp factory; so you don't have to earn a living."

"Fine. I'll join something."

"That's the ticket." Mr. Brumpton folds his magazine and picks up his spoon.

Lydia watches him take a sip of soup. "I'll join the suffragettes."

He spits out his soup.

Mrs. Brumpton puts her hand to her throat. "All those women marching through the streets, being taken off to jail where there are heaven knows what germs."

"You join the suffragettes," Mr. Brumpton says, slamming down his fist, making the glassware tinkle, "and you can leave this house, leave Robin Hood's Bay—no—you can leave Yorkshire if you join that bunch of trouble-making, rabble-rousing . . . I can't call them ladies, they don't know the meaning of the word, they're—"

"Philip! Not now." Mrs. Brumpton glances over at Adrian and me.

Adrian stares ahead as if the back wall is playing the most fascinating movie of all time.

I can't stop watching them, though.

"But," Lydia pleads, "I need to fill my time with something useful. Oh, it's useless talking. You just don't understand."

Mrs. Brumpton touches Lydia's hand.

"It's not right to discuss your feelings so violently."

Lydia pulls her hand away as if it had been burned.

Mr. Brumpton pushes his soup bowl away. "You'll be going away soon, so that's an end to the matter."

Adrian collects the bowls. This seems to be a cue for Sniff and Snaff to check the rug for bread-roll crumbs.

I stack the bowls into the dumbwaiter, wondering why Mr. Brumpton's so upset that Lydia wants to do something with her life. It doesn't make any sense. Everything's upside down.

Adrian serves the next course, and the next. In between he pours red wine in their glasses. Candlelight sparkles off the crystal. Watching the light, my eyes glaze over and I sway from side to side. This dinner seems to be happening in slow motion. So many courses. And why do they have eat so late? If only I was at home having a PJ day, watching a movie instead of pretending to be in one.

At last the Brumptons leave the dining room with Sniff and Snaff trailing. I rub the back of my aching legs, then clear the table with Adrian. But Mr. Brumpton calls out Adrian's name and he has to go.

I pick up Lydia's untouched pie. She never has to stand. Doesn't even have to do a thing if she doesn't want. But I feel sorry for her, and that's funny when you think she's the one with the princess-perfect life.

I start pulling on the dumbwaiter rope. But after a moment, I stop and hold onto it, spellbound. I'm getting to know the people here, beginning to care, and that's not right. This isn't my home, not my family.

But what can I do?

Every night I come down here and sit in this box. I know every square inch of it. I know that the back panel is covered in long claw-like scratches. I know my hand has to avoid a splintery spot in the far right. And I know the longer I sit here, the more I'm in danger of being discovered. But I wait and wait—folding my knees and jamming my feet on the sides to stop my legs from cramping—but nothing ever happens, nothing. I stare at the empty chute, willing it to give me an answer.

Then a frightening thought crosses my mind.

Am I trapped here for the rest of my life?

SCENERY HELPS

Today it's March, and to keep my mind off the date, Adrian's showing me around, pointing things out: "This is Mr. Brumpton's latest Edison." Or, "This is how I light the gas, see. You have to be careful not to pop a hole in the cloth with your match." Scenery helps me keep up my acting. But with Adrian, I never act. He knows my secret, there's a protective bubble when I'm around him.

In the dining room, he inspects the dumbwaiter, shaking the rope, peering down the chute. Nothing happens. He shrugs. I describe my journey down, but he changes the subject. I push the thought away that he still doesn't believe me, and I follow him to a room I've always been told to skip.

He unlocks the door. Abigail passes by and gives us a friendly nod.

I smile back. "She's so nice, don't you think?"

Adrian nods as he opens the door. "This room," he says, "is used for Christmas and parties."

"Neat."

"No. Untidy."

"No. Neat means . . . oh, forget it."

The sunshine peeps through the gaps in the closed shutters. Apart from a piano pushed against the wall and a rolled-up rug, the room is empty. Adrian lights the gas. The crystal chandelier hisses on, and the smooth wooden floor shimmers like a copper river. Unable to resist, I pull my ankle boots off and take a running slide in my stocking feet.

"Here, you can't do that," Adrian says, though he doesn't sound too convincing.

I skid to a stop by the piano.

Adrian laughs. "You're daft, Sally Soforth," he says, but he takes his shoes off too, and slides across the slippery floor, landing at a spot next to me.

I twist my body into a pirouette, "I'm dancing," I call out.

I stop twirling and collapse onto Adrian. He nearly loses his balance trying to steady me. I give him a push. He slides—straight into Birkett—who sends him flying across the room, and Adrian dodges the piano by a slither.

"My office. Now!" Birkett snaps at me.

I zero in on Adrian's eyes and hold onto them all the way to the door.

* * *

Birkett writes at his desk in his accounting book. I sit in a hard chair opposite. The nib of his ink pen makes a scratching noise. I know his stalling tactic is supposed to make me nervous. But I'm not. I'm upset he hit Adrian across the room.

Birkett places his pen in a box on his desk. "Your behavior today is unacceptable," he begins in his low voice. "Though I cannot say I am surprised."

He closes his inkwell shut with a click.

"I've been watching you at work and it is my belief you are not trying hard enough to finish your duties in a timely fashion. You also don't seem to be able to follow all the rules of the house, so it is my duty to remind you of them, just in case you are in any doubt."

With a long, ink-stained finger he pushes his glasses up the bridge of his sweaty nose.

"You always seem to be late. On top of that you keep forgetting all the items on the afternoon tea tray. It is crucial to the running of an ordered household that . . ." On and on he drones, in a voice that doesn't change rhythm, so I just hear the tune of it and not what he's saying. That is, until I hear Adrian's name.

"Spending time with Merryweather cannot be permitted. You leave me no choice but to make sure you are kept apart. Now, I don't blame him. Boys will be boys. But girls should know their place."

He closes his accounting book.

"However, I will let him go without a character reference if I have to. And without a character—well—he'll find it impossible to work."

"But I don't understand," I protest. "We're just friends."

Birkett holds his hand up. "I find that difficult to believe. The amount of time you spend in his company. You are a maid. You are forbidden a male friend, especially one who works in the house. Those are the rules. I did not make them but we must all follow them, no exceptions. Do I make myself clear?"

"But—" I protest.

He cuts me off. "You argue too much."

I feel my face burning. I've said less than ten words since coming into his stinking office and he calls that arguing too much. I try to say something but he narrows his eyes and the full force of his attitude hits me, and instead of fighting my case, I just nod.

He flicks his hand at the door.

* * *

Adrian's waiting for me. He guides me into the lamp room. "Don't let him mess with your head," he whispers.

"He's watching us."

"Let him. He can't get shot of you. You're Mrs. B.'s blue-eyed girl."

"Not me this time. You. He threatened to let you go without a reference unless we stop hanging out."

Adrian turns away, but I've already seen his worried expression. I feel my protective bubble bursting. I can't survive in 1912 without Adrian.

"Don't mither," he says, reading my mind. "Nowt can keep us apart. Nowt."

LOST DAYS

Birkett keeps tabs on Adrian, finding him lots of outside work or errands to run. At meals we can't so much as glance at each other without him sending Adrian back to his work with his food left to get cold on his plate. And every time I do something wrong he takes it out on Adrian. Clever. He's discovered the one thing that will keep me in line.

DAY ONE—I manage OK. I can go it alone. I'm used to having no friends.

DAY TWO—I convince myself the dumbwaiter will work soon; Adrian was fine before I came, he'll be fine when I leave. And when I'm gone, at least his job will be safe.

DAY THREE—I decide to throw myself into scrubbing the scullery steps, then the front steps, followed by a dustpan-and-brushing of the Brumptons' staircase. Who cares about Adrian? Not me, I think, scraping my knees under Lydia's bed searching for dust bunnies to wipe out.

But the week's nearly over, and I'm all worn out and not thinking straight. Take today. I know I must have made up the fires, cleaned the rooms, had meals. But I can't remember any of it. It's like I'm on autopilot and time keeps standing still.

Now it's night and I'm pacing up and down, waiting for the house to go quiet.

I'm not acting. I'm facing reality.

The only noise is the tapping of the water pipes from the bathroom as Abigail, Gerty and Mrs. Meadowcroft take turns getting ready for bed.

Doors closing: one . . . two . . . three. Silence.

I wrap myself in my robe and take the stairs. I don't remember getting to the Brumptons' dining room, but here I am standing in front of the dumbwaiter. I climb in and wait. The cold air and my thoughts make me shiver. I shift my position, forgetting to avoid the rough spot. My hand doesn't hurt that much, so why am I banging the sides with my feet?

"Sally, Sally, what's got into you?" Adrian's staring down at me.

"It won't work," I yell, in between thuds.

He tries to grab my feet. "I can hear thee downstairs."

"I don't care."

"Birkett will hear." Adrian manages to stop me mid-kick.

I cover my face with my hands. "Why won't it work?"

"What? I'm flummoxed on that score, Sally."

I want to tear the thing apart. Instead, I start shaking the rope.

"Come on, let's go. You'll be jiggered in morning."

"I'm not going until it works."

Adrian rubs his eyes. "I don't want you . . ."

"What?" I stop shaking the rope.

He looks into my eyes, but I can't figure out what he's thinking in the dark.

"I don't want you to go," he says. "The dumbwaiter, if it works, then you'll go."

A knife-like pain stabs at my head. "But I can't live here without you."

"I've been thinking along the same lines, but what can we do?"

"Do something," I say, not meaning to sound so harsh but sounding it all the same.

And he walks away. He actually walks away.

With one fluid movement I jump down from the dumbwaiter and back into my movie. What camera was I on? Ah, yes. There it is, blinking red.

Reality?

Way too hard.

NEW DAY

Adrian devises a secret code.

Our Secret Code

Spoon on the scratched table, upside-down: We sneak off to the STABLES

Knife pointing to the door: We meet on the DONKEY PATH

We have to be very, very careful with our silverware scheme. Birkett's no fool, and we must wait until he's not around. But it's worth it. The donkey path gives us a quick getaway to the village if we want to, and the stables are our new favorite place to hang out. And as Adrian says, Old Jack, the coachman, pays us no mind.

* * *

At lunch, I turn my spoon upside-down. Adrian shakes his head in Birkett's direction. Disappointed we won't be going to the stables, I finish my rice pudding.

The bells on the kitchen wall have been quiet.

Mr. Brumpton's in his study. I could smell his cigar smoke coming under the door.

Mrs. Brumpton is out shopping in Scarborough and has taken Abigail with her. I don't know where Lydia is.

It's Gerty's day off, and now lunch is over, I have to wash the dishes. I'm all alone but don't feel lonely. Not now me and Adrian are back spending stolen moments together.

I fill the deep scullery sink with soapy water and swirl some soda crystals in, the way I've been told to. Ouch! These housework scratches never seem to have time to heal. Mr. Brumpton's interested in inventions. Perhaps I'll tell him about dishwashers.

"Pop quiz: Need a hand there?"

"Adrian!"

"Aye, I've escaped. So pass me that towel."

Pretending not to be pleased, I throw a dish towel at his head. He laughs, then starts drying dishes for me. I glance out the window. I'm glad Adrian's here, but I hate the scullery. It's always cold and damp and full of beetles. "It's supposed to be the weekend and we're stuck inside washing dishes."

Adrian picks a dripping cup up and rubs it with his towel. "There's no weekend in service."

"Yeah. Tell me about it. Where's Birkett?"

"He's visiting his ma and won't be back till dark."

We both stop and exchange looks.

"Are you thinking what I'm thinking?" I ask.

"The stables?" Adrian says.

We hurry up and finish. I pull my apron and cap off; Adrian goes to change his footman's uniform; then we both run out the scullery door and up the scullery steps.

It's a gloomy looking Saturday, but at the thought of fooling Birkett, I feel bright and bubbly inside. "Even Old Jack's mood won't spoil our day now."

"Aye, he's a grumpy old codger," Adrian says.

"How old is he?"

"Old enough for new pension but won't take it. Says he's not havin' no charity."

I push open the stable door and squeeze through.

Old Jack is in the end stall, brushing down Copper: a chestnut horse with kind eyes. "Good girl," Old Jack soothes, brushing short, strong strokes down Copper's back. This horse thing is new to me, and I love it.

"You've got Copper's coat proper shiny," Adrian says.

Old Jack looks up with his dark eyes. I always think they can see right through me. I always think Old Jack knows exactly who I am.

"What you two young 'uns up to? Standin' there as cozy as Sniff and Snaff."

Adrian feeds Copper a sugar cube from his pocket. "Just takin' a break."

Old Jack swaps brushes. Copper lets him gently brush her face. The stables are peaceful and smell nice. I ask Adrian what the smell is. "Saddle soap," he says after thinking for a moment. "And clean hay."

Adrian holds his hand out to help me climb the square steps of hay piled in the corner. I brush his hand aside and climb up on my own. We both sit down on the top bale and pull out strands to chew on.

"Who you getting Copper ready for?" Adrian asks, his hay bouncing as he speaks.

Old Jack doesn't look up. "I'm getting 'er ready for master. Not that it's any business of yours, Adrian Merryweather."

Adrian turns to me. "Mr. Brumpton's only person Old Jack likes."

"'E's a grand man," Old Jack agrees. "None better in whole o' Yorkshire."

"But there's one thing about him you're not so keen on," Adrian says in a teasing voice.

Old Jack sniffs. "What's he want to bother hisself with all

this new-fangled codswallop? Nowt wrong with old way of doin' stuff."

Adrian points his hay in my direction. "You don't want Sally thinking us backwards. Mr. Brumpton's replacin' his carriage with a motorcar soon."

Old Jack glares at Adrian. "And where's he going to drive it? Donkey path? Bay's cobbles?" His black eyes turn even blacker. "Na. 'Tis just a flash-in-the-pan, that there horseless carriage. 'Twill never catch on."

"Don't fret," Adrian says. "You'll upset Copper."

But Old Jack won't be sidetracked. "Yon engine—dirty, nasty thing—always breakin' down."

"How do you know?" Adrian asks.

"I'm not so out of it, lad, that I don't know what's going on!" Copper takes a step backwards. Old Jack calms her, saying, "There now. There now. Master'd never get shot of thee." He strokes the horse's face. "Besides," he whispers, "machines don't have hearts."

Adrian looks down at the stable floor. "Nay mind," he says, all the teasing gone from his voice. "Your job's safe for now."

In the awkward silence, Adrian takes out his watch and glances at the time. "Let's go to Ma Thompson's."

I hesitate; Old Jack might disapprove.

"Don't worry about Old Jack," Adrian says, reading my thoughts. He turns to the old man. "You won't let on to Birkett?"

Old Jack grunts, "That worm in me apple." And he spits on the stable floor.

Adrian laughs, Old Jack gives him a half smile, and the awkward atmosphere dissolves.

"I told ya," Adrian says to me. "No one likes Birkett."

We jump down off the hay and give Copper a farewell pat.

Old Jack gathers up his brushes and glances out the rear stable door.

"Don't be long, you two," he warns. "I reckon there's a storm brewin'."

I glance back and see Old Jack's dark eyes burning right through me. "Aye," he says, turning to Copper. "I can feel it in me bones."

THE CALM

A gray mist swirls over the open meadows. I gaze up at the heavens. Eerie how quiet it is. Not even a bird in the sky.

At Ma Thompson's, I order chocolate fudge for me. Hard toffee for Adrian. Adrian also buys a quarter pound of soft toffee for Old Jack. Guilt-toffee, I call it.

Outside, leaning against the red water pump, I nibble on my chocolate fudge. "Let's go exploring."

Adrian agrees, so we go poking our noses into every little alleyway, every little store.

We run down to the Lifeboat House. Three fishermen are leaning on the wall, their thumbs tucked into their belts. I turn my gaze to the cottages around us.

"You looks happy," Adrian says.

"I've just figured something out."

I point to a cottage backyard about the size of my attic room. "Look at this." Weeds are pushing up between the cobblestones and there's a rusty old bathtub hanging by a nail on the cottage wall.

"Nowt special," Adrian says, looking confused. "Just someone's back of house."

"Not just any back of house, as you call it. An *English* one. When my hand touches a door, it's not just any door—it's an *English* door. When my boots touch the ground—it's on *English* ground. I breathe the air and—it's *English* air. I hear a seagull—it's an *English* seagull . . ."

"I gets it," Adrian says, holding his hand up. "We're in England and everything is *Eng-lish*."

"Well, it feels special, that's all. Imagine if you were in America."

"That'd be amazin'."

"Right, so imagine it."

He starts bouncing around touching things. "Ooh, an *American* door. Ooh, an *American* gate. Ooh, an *American* cobble."

While Adrian's making fun of me, I spot Lydia walking towards us in a white hat with a red ribbon round the brim. Too late, she sees us.

"Hello," she says, smiling.

Adrian touches his cap. "Afternoon, Miss," he says, as if we bump into her in Robin Hood's Bay all the time. "Shopping?" He glances down at the cardboard box in her gloved hands.

Lydia lifts the box and shows us the colorful fat elf painted on it. "I'm trying my hand at photography. Mother suggested it. She says it'll take my mind off joining the suffragettes." Lydia gives me a knowing smile, as if I'm planning on joining them too.

"A Number Two Brownie!" Adrian exclaims in the same voice as a Hogwarts' wizard would shout, "A Nimbus 2000!"

Lydia passes Adrian the box with the funny elf on it. He pulls out a cube-shaped camera. It's such a low-tech looking thing, I can't imagine it ever taking a photo.

"The man in the shop says the film even loads in daylight." Lydia turns her friendly eyes on me. "Now Father isn't the only one in the house with the latest thing."

Looking reluctant, Adrian hands the camera back.

Lydia smiles at him. "Would you two oblige me by being the first to have your picture taken?"

Adrian's face brightens. But I'm not so sure. Should I even be having my photograph taken? A girl from the future in a photograph from the past.

Lydia searches for a good spot and we end up outside Ma Thompson's. She takes a photo of Adrian at the red water pump. But Adrian being Adrian he can't just pose naturally. He has to lean to one side and stick his thumbs in his belt, as if he's practicing to be a fisherman.

Lydia snaps a couple more of him, then we move up the street and she positions me in front of the bicycle shop.

"No," I tell her. "Take another of Adrian."

"Don't be silly. You look like a Kodak Girl."

While I wait for her to step back and point the camera, the wind picks up and blows my hair about. I try to flatten it down, but it's still flying in my face when she takes the shot.

Lydia takes a couple more of us, and then we leave her happily snapping away as we head for the beach.

THE STORM

The wind, stronger now, tugs at our clothes and rolling dark clouds tumble towards us. Adrian finds us an over-hanging rock by the cliffside and it protects us from the first drops of rain.

"We should get back," I tell him, as the waves come crashing down. But the drama of it is exciting. That is until the tide begins to turn.

"We're stuck!" I shout above the noise of the wind and the rain and the sea. And the only way to get back to the steps is to wade through the waves.

"This way," Adrian calls, holding his hand out to help me again.

"Stop treating me like a girl in 1912."

"You are a girl in 1912."

He edges away against the cliff wall, reaches the mouth of a cave, and then disappears.

I follow him. The cave narrows into a tunnel. He's nowhere in sight, so trying hard not to slip or worry about what lies ahead, I duck and make my way over the wet uneven rocks.

The light fades into nothingness. Now I'm in swirling black. I wish Adrian hadn't left me. I'm too spooked to go back, and I can't see my way ahead. And there are noises. Dripping water, and every three seconds a frightening booming sound that, after a few seconds, I realize must be the sea smashing against the tunnel walls.

"Ya there?" Adrian's voice echoes down the tunnel.

"Coming," I call out in the dark, trying to keep the fear from my voice.

I take a few faltering steps. The ground slips under my boots and I fall sideways against the scraping rocks. Struggling to stand, I press one hand on the tunnel to steady myself. "Aaargh!" Something wet and slimy with feathery legs touches my hand. That does it. I scramble out fast.

Now I'm at the base of three carved out stone steps. Adrian's standing at the top.

"You left me."

"I thought you wanted me to."

"But not in the dark. I hate the dark."

"I knew where you were." He shoulders a trapdoor. It takes three tries but he manages to heave it open.

As the light hits the tunnel wall, I see a sparkly section of rock. I reach up and touch its prickly surface. I wonder what it's made of.

* * *

On the other side of the trapdoor is the inside of a cottage.

"Uncle Thaddeus," Adrian says, pointing to a photograph on the wall of a fisherman standing outside the front door. And I notice the door is in two parts, and the top part has an anchor carved into it. Except for his height, and his beard, Uncle Thaddeus looks like a weatherworn version of Adrian.

I glance around.

"He's away at sea," Adrian says.

He throws me a rough towel, and I squeeze out my dripping hair with it, focusing on the tiny room we're

THE STORM

standing in. Apart from two stools and a table, there's a sea chest standing in the corner. On the mantel is a pipe and two candles next to a pink pearly seashell. The rain-splashed window has fishing nets for drapes.

I point towards a loft ladder, propped against an opening in the ceiling.

Adrian touches the ladder. "One room up; one room down."

"And a tunnel underneath."

"Lots of cottages are connected by tunnels," he says, as if it were no big deal.

I shiver in the cold. "What would your uncle say about me being here?" I'm feeling surprised to be here myself.

Adrian crouches down to light the wood fire and it crackles alive. "He'd ask you where's your shawl."

I grip the towel round my shoulders as if it were a shawl.

"Then he'd point his pipe at you: 'Your cardigan's no good,' he'd say. 'You should at least have thee a thick jumper.'"

I don't understand. "How can a sleeveless dress keep me warm?"

Adrian plucks at the edge of his sweater. "Nay, 'tis a woolen gansey, see, like this one."

"Well, you know I don't speak Yorkshire." I pick up the pipe off the mantle and sniff it. Yuk. Not like Mr. Brumpton's sweet smelling cigars.

Adrian sees me. "There's a hole in me uncle's tooth where his pipe rests."

I peer at the photograph on the wall but can't make out his uncle's tooth. "Is your uncle away all the time on his boat? Even in winter."

"Aye. He says it's not natural being cooped up inside." Adrian smiles sadly. The wind howls outside. "I don't want to go to sea."

And I know he's thinking about his drowned dad.

He takes out his pocket watch, shakes it, and puts it to his ear. "Me uncle says I should at least find a place away from Birkett. But I told him, there's no other fancy houses round here, and even if there were, I wouldn't go. Look what happened to Gerty."

I'm about to ask him what happened to Gerty, when he throws me a pair of fisherman's overalls. "Get dry upstairs." And he picks up the teakettle.

* * *

We decide to wait until the storm has settled. Both wearing pairs of Uncle Thaddeus's overalls, finishing a hot gravy-tasting drink called Bovril, and snuggled in these two squashy armchairs, we watch the shifting shapes of the fire's burning embers.

Adrian peers at me through drooping eyelids. "Penny for 'em."

"Umm?"

"Penny for your thoughts." He sets his mug on the wood floor.

"Why've we never been here before?"

"I dunno," Adrian says, squirming in his chair. "Not exactly grand like the manor, is it?"

"I'd take this cottage over ten Brumpton Manors."

"Most folk wouldn't agree."

"Most folk are stupid, then."

"Happen." And he closes his eyes.

I ignore his closed eyes. "You'd miss it if you had to go away."

He stirs and mumbles something about America.

"What happened to Gerty?"

"Hmm?"

"You said something happened to Gerty."

"Maid-of-all-work. Blacksmiths. Never fed her." He turns

his head into the chair. "Skin and bone she were." And he falls asleep.

"Poor Gerty," I whisper to the fire.

Draining back my drink, I ease out of my chair, tiptoe over to the table, and lift one of the wooden stools. I carry it to the fireplace and hang over our wet clothes to dry. Now I light the candles on the mantel. Adrian still doesn't stir, even at the sound of the striking match.

Over at the window, I push back the fishing-net drapes. The rain is falling onto the cobblestones. They glisten in the moonlight.

Suddenly, I have this flashback to one of my first days here. I'm peering down from my attic window, wondering what the village is like. Not in a million years would I have imagined I'd be here, in one of these red-roofed cottages with a footman from the house.

I close my eyes.

And picture everyone from 1912. Servants, Brumptons, Adrian. All standing at my left side. My right side is empty. Dad and Mom and Gran are missing. In their place is a shadow, resting on my shoulder.

For weeks now, I've tried to push my other life out. But for once, I give myself permission to remember. I try to picture Gran's face. But I can't see her face.

Why can't I see her face?

I'm about to panic, when I hear her coughing and her face comes into view. She's getting ready for Bingo. Trying to win me theme park tickets. I picture her tidying the house before she goes. Making it as nice as she can. I don't care now that the furniture's shabby and the drapes are faded and . . . was it too late to realize that it didn't matter what type of house I lived in, as long as Gran lived there too?

No. No. No.

It can't be too late. And with a stab of guilt I realize I haven't been near the dumbwaiter at night. Not for ages now. Haven't even thought about it. I close the fishing-net drapes and make a decision.

I'll go there tonight.

SHINING LIGHT

We sprint back to the house, still in overalls, our footwear wet and squelchy.

"I'll go in first," Adrian says, as we hide behind the scullery wall. "When it's safe, I'll wave me lamp."

I watch him sneak up to the house. On the way, he picks up a bucket of coal. "Aye, lad," I say to the wall, talking like a Bay girl to see how it feels. If he bumps into Birkett, he'll need an excuse.

Adrian's light sways in the scullery window, and I dart into the house. He rushes over and passes me his lantern, holding his finger to his lips to warn me to keep quiet.

Remembering first to take off my boots, I dash up our stairs, smiling to myself. They never take off their shoes in the movies when they're trying to keep quiet. Why is that?

Up in my room, I peel off the borrowed overalls, pull my night things on, and jump into bed. Abigail bursts in, and I nearly scream.

"Eee, where've you been in this dirty weather?" she hisses, her voice sounding like a Bay girl for a change too. "I had to do the dishes."

"Sorry," I say, meaning it. "We went out and ended up getting caught by the tide."

Abigail starts fiddling with her blonde hair in the dresser

mirror. "You can't just go out as you please," she says, returning to her careful speech pattern. "You have to grow up sometime."

I spot the overalls on the floor.

Oops! I reach down and slide them under the bed.

Abigail turns and smiles. "What a day! I thought I was going to get blown in the sea."

"How was Scarborough?" I ask. "Did you help Mrs. Brumpton with her shopping?"

"I'd rather go on my own."

"What did you buy?"

"Oh, luggage and some of her headache powder." Abigail sits on my bed. "Where'd you get that lamp?"

"It's Adrian's."

"It's nice you two are friends. I don't have friends. Not in this pokey village." She frowns. "You know, I never understood why you came here from the south. You could've gone anywhere instead of this place—you could've gone to London." She stares out my window as if imagining London out there in the dark.

"What's so special about London?" I ask, feeling loyal all of a sudden to Robin Hood's Bay.

"London?" she says, still staring out the window. "Motorcars, music halls, Buckingham Palace."

"The Queen," I add.

She snaps out of her window staring. "What century are you living in? There's a king on the throne."

"Have you been to London?" I ask, trying to cover up my mistake.

"No," she says, pouting. "*Women's Weekly* did this day-trip thing."

"Oh." And I get this image of one of my movie posters at home. Peter Pan flying around Big Ben. It hangs next to Mary Poppins, umbrella floating over a London sky.

"I'm not always going to be a maid, you know." She leans forward, and I can smell the lemons in her blonde hair.

"Can you keep a secret?"

I nod and smile. If only she knew.

"One day." She pauses dramatically. "I'm going to be an actress."

"An actress?"

"Yes. I've been taking elocution lessons. Can't you tell?" She smiles. "I've got to, if I want to go on the stage or—now don't be shocked—go to America and be in the pictures like Mary Pickford." And she unfolds from her apron pocket a crumpled newspaper clipping of an actress with long, long curls and dramatic silent-movie eyes.

Go to America, I repeat in my head. Be in the pictures. And a wonderful warm glow fills my body and a piece of my life slots into place. I can almost hear the sound of it.

Act.

I want to act.

"You do look shocked," Abigail says.

The need to share is strong, but I don't want to steal her limelight. "What? No, it's great."

"If I had the money, I'd go right now. I'd walk out the front door and never come back."

"I'd like to see Birkett's face if you do."

"Oooh, the precious front door. We mustn't walk through it or germs will attack Mrs. Brumpton and the end of the world will come."

We both laugh.

Abigail stands and smoothes out the creases of her uniform. "Well, it's getting late," she says, turning to leave. She stops at the door. "Don't forget my tea tomorrow." And walks out.

I flop back on my pillow and sigh.

An actress? Well, haven't I been acting all along? I smile up at the slanted ceiling. I'll be able to do period pieces anyway. I pull the covers over my shoulders and imagine I'm up there on the stage, giving my acceptance speech for the Academy Award I've just received ...

I'd like to thank the director and the screenwriter and all the wonderful people who helped make this movie. Oh, and I mustn't forget Adrian Merryweather, my co-star. Thank you, Adrian. And finally, a big thanks to all the people on location in Robin Hood's Bay—this one's for you.

For a few minutes I savor my warm glow. The rain starts up again, tap-tap-tapping on my window. I know the sea's out there, and the village, and Uncle Thaddeus's fisherman's cottage: one room up; one room down. I know Adrian's downstairs, locking up the house, safe and sound.

I close my eyes. "Tomorrow," I murmur, in that Peter Pan place between sleep and awake. "I'll go to the dumbwaiter tomorrow."

FORGETTING WHERE I AM

The sky outside looks as if someone has turned down the sun. Opening the morning-room door, I scratch at the wall for a light switch.

No electricity. I still forget.

The gaslights aren't lit, so I go build up the fire.

Mrs. Brumpton strides in, filling the air with her perfume. Old Sniff and Snaff are trying to keep up.

"Go ahead, Sally, don't mind me," she says.

She sweeps past in her long black skirt, takes a seat in her high-back chair and gives me a pleased-to-see-my-war-on-dirt-in-action look.

I move over to the wall with my maid's cleaning box and start dusting the flower-shaped speaker on the Edison, keeping one eye on Mrs. Brumpton.

Sniff and Snaff perk their ears up and stare at the door.

Mr. Brumpton walks in with his head down, as if he's got something on his mind. He doesn't notice me, so I keep quiet and listen. "My dear," he says, leaning one elbow on the fireplace, "seeing as you refuse to have an electrical generator."

"Wait until the village has one," Mrs. Brumpton interrupts.

Mr. Brumpton sighs. "I could try so many inventions with electricity."

"I don't know what for."

"I could get you the latest cleaning machines."

"Are you suggesting I become a servant in my own home?"

"That's not what I said. I'm just trying to bring us into the twentieth century."

Mrs. Brumpton clutches at her skirt. "Electricity's unreliable and dangerous. Why waste money?"

Mr. Brumpton stares into the fire and sighs again. "Electricity is the future . . . that's why I'm worried about the factory." He mumbles these last words and Mrs. Brumpton doesn't hear them.

"We'll start the spring cleaning soon," she says.

I glance at the duster in my hand. Pop quiz: What's this "we" business, she's talking about?

Mr. Brumpton nods and helps himself to a fat cigar from a box on the mantel. "Why can't we have the spring cleaning done while we're away?"

"I like to oversee it."

"Well, I think it should be done when we're in New York—"

"You're going to America!" I shriek.

Mr. Brumpton drops his cigar in the fire. "Where did she spring from?"

"Oh, Sally, I forgot you were there," Mrs. Brumpton says. "Yes, we're going on a trip. But don't you worry, Mrs. Meadowcroft will be in charge while we're away."

"Isn't the butler in charge?"

"We'll be taking Birkett with us. Now if you've finished."

My mind jumps three thousand miles across the sea. "Are you going to visit all the tourist sights?"

"What sights are those, dear?" Mrs. Brumpton asks.

"Oh, you know, places like the Empire State Building."

"Where's that?"

I quickly backtrack. "I mean the Statue of Liberty."

I cross my fingers that it's been built.

"No doubt we'll see it from the ship," she says.

Oh, yeah. A ship. They won't be flying—no jumbo jets. I think back to one of my history classes. All the immigrants' stories. "You'll probably see Ellis Island. Ships used to—I mean, have to—stop there. You may need a medical exam."

"Ellis Island? No, dear," Mrs. Brumpton says. "We're going first class. Now you really must let Mr. Brumpton and I finish our conversation."

But Mr. Brumpton is staring at me. "You seem to know a lot about America. Have you been there?"

He's never spoken directly to me before, and I feel as if an actor's jumped off the screen in the middle of a movie and started talking.

"Umm, yes, sir . . . I mean . . . no, sir."

"Well, what *do* you mean?"

I decide to invent something. "My aunt lives there and writes me about it."

"Writes *to* me, Sally. Not writes me," Mrs. Brumpton corrects.

Mr. Brumpton relaxes.

"Ah, wonderful country—America—full of superb people with first-class ideas. Especially Mr. Edison." He takes another cigar from the box, lights it, and blows smoke at the ceiling. "And the buildings they're constructing. I hear one's as high as fifteen floors . . ."

Mrs. Brumpton looks over at me and nods towards the door. The sound of Mr. Brumpton's voice follows me all the way down the hall, up the Brumptons' stairs and past Abigail on her way down.

Using a small brush from my box, I start sweeping the stair carpet on my hands and knees. Repetitive work that allows my mind to drift. Far away. To America, and the Brumptons' vacation. I try to imagine New York in 1912. No skyscrapers. No yellow cabs. No Empire State Building.

What if I went with them? Would I escape to Florida? Go to Orlando?

"Ah, well," I mumble, sweeping the sand and dust and dog hair off the last step. "What good would that do?"

"Clean apron, girl!" Birkett's creepy voice hits me on the back of the head.

Bruce Almighty!

Will he stop doing that!

THE BIRDS

This morning the seagulls woke me too early and I couldn't get back to sleep. It's not good when that happens; there's too much time to think. Now Birkett keeps bugging me. Clean this. Clean that. I try to avoid him, but he always seems to know where I am.

"Mr. and Mrs. Brumpton have left the house," he's telling me now. "So you can let the morning-room fire go out."

Good. That fire eats coal like Calcifer the fire demon.

He remembers something and his face doesn't approve. "Miss Lydia wants to take a photograph of all the servants. We're to line up at the front of the house, so for heaven's sake, make yourself presentable."

* * *

The weather is behaving for Lydia. Just before she clicks her camera, I turn round on the steps and check out the other servants. Adrian's flattened his curls down with water, and I try not to laugh. He looks really serious and so does everyone else.

"We'll look a miserable bunch when that comes out," I tell him, lifting Smudge into my arms.

"Never heard of 'smile for the camera'?" I ask.

Adrian shakes his head.

We all head to the back of the house, through the scullery and into the wash-house. Everyone except me marvels at the new washing machine Mr. Brumpton's just had delivered. I'm tired and not in the mood. But I suppose the winding handle's one up from scrubbing.

"Now all we need is a machine to do the dishes," I tell Gerty at lunch.

"Oh, Sally." She laughs. "You don't want me out of a job, do ye?"

I wouldn't mind, I think, glaring at the back of Birkett's greasy head. But to spare her feelings, I keep quiet.

Birkett glances over at me, and just to get back at him, I turn my spoon upside down—our code for the stables.

* * *

Old Jack is in the stable-yard cleaning the carriage and whistling a tune. He almost looks happy. Taking a pitchfork off the stable floor, I start prodding at the hay bales. Copper watches me under her eyelashes.

"What's up with thee?" Adrian asks, leaning back on our hay bales.

"What's up?" I throw the pitchfork down. "Apart from getting up at stupid-o'clock, you mean."

He laughs. "Aye. Apart from that."

"I'm tired of carrying coal up and Mr. Brumpton sitting there watching the fire go out."

"Yesterday you were moaning he didn't use the shoe scraper."

"Well, he didn't."

"Six weeks ago you didn't know what a shoe scraper was."

"What's that to do with owt?" I yell, turning Yorkshire in my anger.

"I suppose in your time he'd send you to the Grand Hotel for a rest. No wonder I wouldn't mind going back with you. People sitting around all day with nothing to do."

I try hard to be patient. After all, he is a hundred years behind the time. "Look, in my time everyone helps. In regular homes they do, anyway."

"Everyone?" Adrian looks at me as if I've turned into E.T. "Even men o' the house?"

"Men aren't from another planet. They even change diapers. I bet the men here haven't even heard of diapers."

"What's diapers?"

"Exactly."

"But—"

"No buts. Even my dad, who had nightshifts at his warehouse job, did his share. And not just because my mom died." I walk over to Copper and bury my face in her soft mane. I don't feel like arguing any more.

"Your ma died? You never said."

In all our talks, I've never told him. Only about Dad. How he had toxic shock after his appendix was removed. Routine operation, they'd said. But something had gone wrong when Dad came home. "Doctors," he'd groaned to Gran that last day. "Who's got money for more doctors?" And Gran had banged the pans in the sink, and I'd hidden in my room in my movies and I never got to say goodbye.

I rub my cheek against Copper's warm face and push my feelings down.

Adrian goes quiet for a heartbeat, then says, "I understand if you don't want to talk about your ma."

"I never talk about her."

"Oh?"

"She died when I was a baby. It was an accident—" I lift my head up. "What's that noise?"

We both listen. Even Copper pricks up her ears.

"Stable clock," Adrian says as the clock strikes ten.

"No. Listen."

It's a sound I haven't heard for a long, long time, and we both run outside to Old Jack. I watch with my mouth open as Mr. Brumpton, with Mrs. Brumpton next to him, comes driving through the side entrance in a nail-polish red car, 1912 style. He turns the steering wheel towards the front of the house and tosses the end of a cigar on the ground as he passes.

Old Jack, holding onto his bucket of muddy water, stares at the dying cigar. "I don't believe it. I don't believe it," is all he can say. He throws his bucket to the ground and the muddy water splashes over his clean carriage wheels.

"Did you know Mr. Brumpton was picking up a car today?" I ask Adrian.

He shakes his head. "I would have warned Old Jack, if I had."

Old Jack storms off.

Adrian looks sad. "I never thought it'd bother me so much. Copper being replaced by a motorcar."

"Not me. I knew it would get to me."

"Why?"

But I won't answer him. I won't tell him that my mom never saw the car that hit her. Never saw the red-light runner as she tried to cross the road. No. I don't want to see a car come here any more than Old Jack does.

I drag my feet back to the house.

Birkett's at the scullery door. Abigail standing behind him. "In here, now!" he demands, but I don't really care.

I look back for Adrian and see a black-and-white magpie perched on the wall.

One for sorrow.

MR. BRUMPTON'S STUDY

The rain sloshing about the scullery yard, pouring down the drains and overflowing Ned's water barrels makes me think of Adrian. He's on his way to the village, getting soaked without an umbrella. Perhaps I can meet him for lunch at the tea shop and take him one.

Before I get the chance, Abigail pulls me to one side. "Give Mr. Brumpton's study a quick lick 'n' a promise, will you?"

"I thought Mr. Brumpton didn't want his stuff disturbed."

"You're experienced now, Sally; I'm busy sorting out Mrs. Brumpton's clothes for her trip."

Well, at least it'll be easy, I think. But when I open Mr. Brumpton's study door and turn up the gaslight, I'm not so sure.

Stuff in Mr. Brumpton's Study
- Stack of car magazines
- Cornflakes with "TRY THESE" written on the box
- Drawings of: elevators, escalators and subways
- Three typewriters
- Five cameras—one on its own tripod

- Four models of Edison and two models of Victrola gramophones
- Three gadgets with Edison stamped on them (no clue what they do)
- Teabags with "SAMPLE" written on the box
- One teddy bear

Except for the top of the car magazine stack and the keys of the typewriters, I daren't clean a thing. And I can't do the floor. There's no floor showing. And I can't polish the desk. There's no space on that either.

But over in the corner, next to the camera on a tripod, is another smaller desk with a flip-down top. There's nothing on it but a vase of wilting red tulips. At least I can polish that. I edge my way over, take the beeswax polish from my maid's cleaning box and start rubbing.

Bruce Almighty!

I catch the vase mid-fall. It doesn't break. But vase-water splashes all over the desk lid, seeps down the sides and disappears. I slide open the lid, making even more water pour onto a pile of rolled-up papers. I take my duster and dab at the mess. I unroll one paper but make it worse—smudging ink, wiping out pencil.

I stop.

And stare.

At a drawing of a dumbwaiter.

Is it part of the house plans?

There's a message at the top, written in swirly handwriting: *The thing I lose patience with the most is the clock—its hands move too fast. Merry Christmas, Thomas A. Edison.*

What! Merry Christmas from who?

Edison!

Mr. Brumpton actually knows him!

My heart thumping, I take the dripping document over to

the gaslight and study the drawing. The dumbwaiter has arrows marked over it, pointing to circles and coils and a network of squiggly lines. There are side notes about a portal, and underneath, jagged shapes.

What does this drawing mean? Did Mr. Brumpton and Edison turn the dumbwaiter into my time machine? Or are they going to in their future, and I've fallen down it into their past?

My head buzzes trying to figure it all out. And my arms are getting tired, so I take the drawing over to Mr. Brumpton's big desk and spread it out on top of his clutter.

My finger follows the longest wavy line, all the way down the page until I reach the writing at the end: *For instructions go to,* then it says—what does it say? The words are faded, and what with the water splashes—oh, that's it—*second page.*

The door opens, and I scramble to roll the drawing up.

"Here you are." It's Adrian, his curls wet with rain.

"Don't do that! I thought it was Birkett."

"Birkett's in his office. Writing out our spring-cleaning list."

"Come and see this." I wave him over. "Quick."

I unroll Edison's drawing again. Adrian pores over it, his eyes get wider and wider.

"What d'you make of it?" I ask.

"It explains a lot."

"Does it?" I rub my forehead.

"Edison. He's gone and invented your time machine."

Thomas Edison. Wow. He's not just a name in a history book. He's still alive. Still inventing. He knows Mr. Brumpton. May even have been in this house. This very room.

"All this time Mr. Brumpton had this drawing." I bang my hand on a typewriter, making its bell ring. "Oh why did I have to ruin it?"

Adrian looks up. "I never really believed," he mumbles.
"What's that?" I ask.
"Not really. Time travel. Just too incredible."
"You must have thought I was loopy." I pick up the teddy bear and give it a hug.
"No. Just thought it were our game."
"Nice."
He looks at me with his honest gray eyes. "It wasn't nice. But . . ."
"Forget it. Let's focus on this now." I tap the drawing.
Adrian nods.
I point to the line about the second page.
"I'll help you look for it." He searches Mr. Brumpton's big desk and the piles of stuff scattered on the floor. I go back to the small desk and rummage though that.
No luck.
But I do find a letter from Edison to Mr. Brumpton about them meeting up in Robin Hood's Bay. Edison really did come here and make my time machine, and Mr. Brumpton was in on it.
We rummage for the missing page through the rest of Mr. Brumpton's stuff. But we don't find anything to do with dumbwaiters or secret portals.
"We'd better go," Adrian says, checking his pocket watch.
I carefully roll up Edison's drawing. I want to sneak it to my room and examine every little detail. "At least I've got hope now."
Adrian gives me an encouraging nod. "Don't mither, we'll find that missing page."
But as we leave Mr. Brumpton's study, I notice he looks sad.

MISSING PAGE

The spring cleaning comes in handy.
    For detective work.
    We clean an area; search an area. Opening cupboards. Pulling out drawers. When that doesn't work, we hunt for false bookcases and secret safes, tapping the back of wardrobes or pressing paneling. When we give up doing that, we peel back rugs to check for loose floorboards or trapdoors.
    We turn up—zilch.
    "That page is missing for good," Adrian says, wiping the dust off his footman's jacket.
    "Don't say that. You're not the one missing in the wrong time."
    Birkett strides past on his way to the kitchen, and we try to look busy by looking up at the spring-cleaning list.
    "You'll see your Gran again . . . you will," Adrian says, changing his tone to a supportive one.
    He peers at the list. *Cleanliness is Next to Godliness*, Birkett has written at the top.
    "Can you read out my duties again," Adrian asks. "I'm having trouble with Birkett's handwriting."
    I look at Birkett's perfectly formed but swirly writing.

"No sweat," I say, copying his casual tone. I turn a couple of pages and find his name.

Adrian Merryweather—Footman
Silverware—clean and check for dents.
Take dented items to silversmiths on Silver
Street. Glassware—wash decanters and
water jugs. Knifes—sharpen kitchen knifes
and polish with wellington knife powder.
Lighting—clean gas-lamp fixtures and
chandeliers. Exterior: wash outside
windows. Sweep steps and scullery yard.

Adrian lets out a long, low whistle.

"If you think that's bad," I moan, "you should read mine, it's twice as long." I look down at my sore and swollen hands. "Perhaps I'll run away to Hollywood. Wait for Charlie Chaplin to arrive."

The hurt look Adrian gives me, makes me realize he still doesn't get my jokes.

Birkett's gone to the village, so Adrian decides to take the opportunity to search his office for the missing page. A long shot I know, but we've run out of places to look.

For the rest of the morning, I bite my nails, worrying Birkett will come back and find Adrian. Lucky for me Mrs. Brumpton and Lydia have gone to Scarborough to shop for their American trip.

Abigail pops her head in the drawing room where I'm pretending to clean. "I'm taking my afternoon off. Do the tea for me later, will you?"

"Sure."

"Positive."

"I mean, I will. Have a nice day."

She smiles and hurries out the room.

At lunch, Adrian's late, and I can't touch a bite. Also, it's rabbit stew. Rabbits are pets not food.

At last Adrian joins us at the scratched table when we're sipping our tea. He points his spoon upside down—twice—just to make sure I've got the message.

I run to the stables. Old Jack's not there. Or Copper. But I can see Copper in the meadow, enjoying the sun now the rain's gone.

Adrian's waiting. "I've found summat," he says. He looks at my face. "No. Not the missing page." He passes me a piece of paper. It's a letter, full of spelling mistakes

> *Deer Lady,*
>
> *I thawt you shud naw yon Sally who is imployed by your kind self has a deadly dis-ease called Consumsion.*
>
> *Germs are jumping from her to thems arownd.*
>
> *Yors in trooth,*
>   *A wel wisher*

"What!" I yell. "Who could've written this?"

"Birkett."

"Birkett?"

"He's disguised his writing by using print, but some of the letters are his fancy ones all right. It took me so long to read, I noticed them."

I picture Birkett writing, his mind turning like the cogs and wheels of a clock. "What's"—I read the letter again—'consumsion'?"

"Consumption. TB. Bad lungs. Me ma died of it."

"Birkett's mean."

"Yeah. But he's being stupid. You'd be coughing all over the place if you had it. Coughing blood."

"Oh." I shiver.

Adrian shivers too. He passes me something else. A hardback book. *1912* is written on the cover.

"What's this?" I open it and gasp. It's Birkett's accounting book. "If he finds out it's missing, he'll freak."

"Nay mind that. Take a gander at his writing."

I scan across the columns of numbers all lined up neatly, next to dates and descriptions such as:

3rd March, 4 doz Eggs, Ravenscar Dairy, 3 shillings

I'm no handwriting expert, but I can see what Adrian means. In both sets—the letter and the accounting book—a lot of the writing has the same big swirls.

"I feel sick."

Adrian takes the accounting book and points to our stack of hay bales. "Here, sit thee down."

We climb to our usual spot.

Adrian passes me another piece of paper folded in two. "There's more rum goin's on."

It's another letter. Something falls out and I watch it float to the stable floor. Money. Paper money. Five pounds.

Adrian jumps down and snatches it up, while I read the letter that's written in nearly the same hand as before—Birkett's.

> *Dearest Mother,*
>   *I hope this letter reaches you in good health. Enclosed is £5 to be added to our retirement.*
>   *Hide it in the usual place.*
>   *It's all I can manage this month owing to the added expense the Brumptons have for their trip.*
>   *Fondest wishes, Hiram*

"Pop quiz: What's 'all I can manage this month' mean?"

"Birkett's creaming off the housekeeping. Linin' his own pocket."

"Stealing from the family? The way he's so stingy with our candles." I climb down off the hay and pass the accounting book and letters to Adrian. "What're we going to do?"

"I don't rightly know."

"What if we keep these letters? Stop him sending them?"

Adrian rubs his curls. "He'd just write them out again."

"What if we just show them to Mrs. Brumpton?"

"Birkett could say we'd written them." He taps Birkett's stuff. "I'd better put these back. I have to go. Mr. Brumpton needs me this afternoon to sort some of his clothes."

I stare at the five pounds. It'd take me five backbreaking months to earn that much. Longer, with my uniform deduction. "I'll put them back."

And who knows what else I'll uncover.

TO CATCH A THIEF

Birkett's office is not like Mr. Brumpton's study. There's nothing strewn across the desk or piled up on the floor. Except for his raincoat hanging on a coat hook, the place doesn't even look occupied. It'll make for an easier search, but I'll have to be careful to leave everything exactly the way I find it.

I place the letters and accounting book on his desk. Apart from his pen box and inkwell, there's nothing else to see.

And the drawers are locked.

No amount of pushing and pulling will get them open.

I squeeze behind his desk to get to a cupboard. It's open. I start rifling through his things—books about being a butler, a bottle of ink, a box of assorted keys, even a silver teapot with its handle missing—but there's nothing of interest.

I start straightening everything back to its original place when a noise from outside the door makes me stop. I eye the room frantically for a hiding place. The door rattles. No time to think. I dive behind Birkett's raincoat and wrap it round me like a cloak.

* * *

Holding my breath and listening hard, I try to guess what's going on. I know it's Birkett, I can feel his attitude in the room. A chair scrapes. A jangling—keys I think—now a tapping noise and the sound of a drawer opening. Click. That's his inkwell.

Oh no! Just how long is he staying here?

I command my body not to itch. My nose not to sneeze. Birkett's coat smells of stale sweat, and I try not to gag. Risking it, I push my nose out for air. This gives me a narrow view of his hands on the desk. His spindly fingers are writing on something. An envelope, I think.

Birkett's hand moves across the desk and picks up one of the letters. He pulls out the five pounds, pauses, and tucks it back in. Now he reaches into his drawer and takes another envelope, writes on that, and just as he puts his pen back, someone comes banging through the door and I nearly scream. I press back against the wall and hold my stomach in.

"Knock first," Birkett snaps.

"I did."

Abigail! What's she doing here on her afternoon off?

Unable to resist, I pull the raincoat back a peephole, just in time to see Birkett flipping the envelopes face down. Abigail's in front of his desk. Her arms are crossed. I admire her outfit: a rich burgundy jacket with a matching skirt that touches her shoes.

"I think the girl and Adrian have been sneaking around together again."

What? I cover my mouth with my hand.

"I find that difficult to believe," Birkett says in his low voice. "I've given her enough work to last a month of Sundays."

"Well, why else would she go to the stables?"

"The stables? Better keep an eye on her, then."

"What's in it for me?"

"You can finish work early. When I've left for this trip, mind, we don't want the others to get suspicious."

Memories of Abigail come flooding in. Abigail giving me a warm cardigan. Abigail doing my hair. Confiding in me. Showing me pictures of actresses. All this time she was pretending to be my friend.

I press onto the wall for support.

That's why Birkett kept turning up. He knew because of Abigail. Like that time we were skating across the floor, she'd passed us in the hallway first. Anytime Birkett'd found us, she'd been there somewhere before. Right from my first day.

"Maybe you two can work together," Birkett is saying.

"No. I don't want to scrub floors. You promised," Abigail answers, and I nearly jump out and flatten her.

"Just keep an eye open. Now, can't you see I'm busy?"

Abigail turns to leave.

The door slams, and Birkett sighs. He slots the letters into their envelopes, then tidies his tidy desk and stands to leave. I pull back against the wall, praying my boots are covered. What if he wants his raincoat? I close my eyes and tense my body.

I hear the door closing. Thank heavens for the sunshine today.

Throwing off Birkett's stinking raincoat and, for now, Abigail's deceit, I check his desk. He's taken the envelopes with him.

But he's left his key in the drawer.

I pull the drawer open. I'm not leaving here without looking for the missing page.

Lying on the top of his papers is another accounting book marked 1912.

Why? The other one wasn't full. I snatch it up and flip through the pages. Now I pick the first accounting book off his desk and flip through that. Both seem identical. But not quite. The dates and descriptions are the same—but the totals are different. One of the books has higher amounts.

So that's his game.

He has two sets of books: one real, one fake.

He must pay the bills with the amounts from the real book, but show the fake book with the higher amounts to Mrs. Brumpton and pocket the difference. The slimeball.

Both Abigail and him are slimeballs.

I glance up at the door. Birkett may return any minute, but I can't put his fake accounting book down. A bunch of the entries list the people who call at the house: the milkman, the coal man, the butcher's boy, the baker's boy, the blacksmith. It gives a whole new meaning to delivery. The only thing we ever had delivered in Orlando was pizza. Oh yeah—and the mail—and I picture Birkett down at the red mailbox, dropping his poison letters in.

I flip through the pages of his book. One of the entries catches my eye: *March 30th: Knifeman.* I've never seen a knifeman at the house. I run my finger down two more pages. Here he is again, the first day of our spring cleaning: *Knifeman, sharpen kitchen knives, two shillings and sixpence.* Well, just because I've never seen him, doesn't mean he never visits.

Hold on.

There is no knifeman. Adrian sharpens the knives. It's one of his jobs on Birkett's spring-cleaning list. Talk about sharp goings on. Fake accounting. Fake trades people. Yeah, and probably fake deliveries.

It could be my jumpy imagination, but I think I hear a noise outside the door. I freeze.

The noise goes away.

I drop the books in the drawer and close it. They're not going anywhere.

* * *

Adrian's busy with Mr. Brumpton. I don't see him until supper but we still can't talk in front of Birkett. After supper, Birkett leaves our dining room, and everyone relaxes around the scratched table in small groups, drinking hot chocolate and chatting in hushed voices. Ned's smoking his second cigarette and the room looks like a blurry movie from the black-and-white days.

"Birkett has a spy," I tell Adrian, after first checking over my mug that Abigail is busy talking to Mrs. Meadowcroft.

"I find that difficult to believe," Adrian answers, copying Birkett's annoying catchphrase.

"No, seriously. Don't you ever wonder how he always finds us out?"

"I just thought we had bad luck." Adrian takes his lucky heart-shaped penny from his pocket and twirls it between his finger and thumb.

"Pop quiz: Who in the house never gets into trouble, and who knows where we're going half the time?"

He glances round the table. "Not Old Jack?"

"No. Abigail."

"How'd you find out?"

I explain.

He takes a sip of his hot chocolate. "We'll have to be right careful from now on."

"For real."

I tell him about Birkett's bogus accounting book.

"He'll regret doing it," Adrian says, opening his watch and looking down at the sailing ship.

"Yeah," I agree. "When he gets caught."

He closes his watch. "No."

I give Adrian a second look.

He finishes his hot chocolate and stares into the empty cup. "Down the road. When he thinks back on his life."

I study Adrian's face.

He's a deeper thinker than I thought.

"What're we going to do?" he asks.

"I left Birkett's accounting books in his office. I can go back for them when Mrs. Brumpton comes home from her shopping trip."

Tomorrow.

CRISS-CROSS

Mrs. Brumpton and Lydia burst through the door in a hustle and bustle of hats and coats, packages and bags. Sniff and Snaff come limping down the stairs and Birkett has to dodge round them.

Upstairs, I drop my scrubbing brush into my bucket and shuffle over on my knees to spy at them through the gap in the staircase railing.

Birkett welcomes them home in his sucking-up style. "Post for you, ma'am," he says, holding under Mrs. Brumpton's nose a silver plate piled high with letters.

I bite my bottom lip. He's kept her mail under lock and key all day.

"Not now, Birkett," Mrs. Brumpton answers, pushing away the plate with one hand and passing him her gloves and hat with the other.

They walk past under me, and I pull back, almost knocking my bucket over. The drawing-room door closes. I pick up my brush and start scrubbing again.

Birkett's office light burns late, but Mrs. Brumpton still doesn't ring. I go to bed but I can't sleep. I should have kept those letters when I had the chance.

* * *

After breakfast, the morning-room bell finally rings, and Birkett practically falls over himself running to answer it.

"Well, I never," Mrs. Meadowcroft says, getting up from the kitchen table. "What's he in such a hurry for?"

I feel my stomach muscles tense.

"It's been all go this morning. We've already had the telephone ring."

I check the clock, wondering who could have called before nine.

Mrs. Meadowcroft checks my uniform is tidy. "Run along or you'll have *him* to answer to."

Reluctantly, I haul a rug into the wash-house yard, throw it over the washing line, and begin beating it with the hand rug beater. Right now, I'd give my movie collection for a vacuum cleaner.

"Sally," I hear Abigail call through the wash-house peephole window. "Mrs. B. wants a word."

This is it, then. Mrs. Brumpton's opened her mail. I give the rug an extra thump. The rug chokes me back with sand and dust. I stumble through to the scullery and splash my hands and face in the sink. Gerty passes me her tea towel, and her sympathy. Abigail gives me a what-have-you-done? look.

I ignore her. Partly because I feel sick.

* * *

Sniff and Snaff are both staring up at Birkett.

"Ah, Sally," Mrs. Brumpton says from her high-back chair. "I need to speak to you about something serious."

She's holding a piece of paper.

A letter.

I shoot Birkett a look. He's standing as still as one of her figurines. Mrs. Brumpton coughs. It reminds me of Gran, and I nearly throw-up there and then on her nice clean rug.

"I was opening my post this morning, when I came across this letter—"

"No. No. Mrs. Brumpton," I jump in. "I can explain."

"Can you, Sally? But you don't know what I am referring to."

"I do. I've seen that letter. And other things in Birkett's office. Just ask him. Ask him to show you his accounting books."

"No, Sally. I will not."

"What!" Gerty was right then, a man's job does come first. My stomach twists at the injustice of it, and I glare at Birkett. Why hasn't he defended himself? Is he that confident as the man in charge?

Mrs. Brumpton's voice makes me pay attention.

"I don't need to look at the books. Because I know this letter is a fraud, written in this man's hand."

How does she know Birkett wrote it? Has she spotted his handwriting too?

Mrs. Brumpton folds the letter neatly in half. "I couldn't understand it at first, but then I realized that I'd been sent it by mistake. You see, this letter was supposed to go to this man's mother. The contents inform me that he is a thief. I won't read it out, but the proof is inside."

I open my mouth but nothing comes out. Just what letter is she talking about?

She folds the letter again. "Earlier this morning, I received an interesting telephone call from this man's mother. After I got over the shock of her owning a telephone, I listened. She said she'd received a letter sent to her by mistake. One that was meant for me."

I look again at Birkett. His skin's the color of candle wax. He even looks like he's melting.

"At first I was confused," Mrs. Brumpton continues. "Then it occurred to me. It's a simple mistake. After he wrote these letters, he put them in the wrong envelopes."

The room wobbles.

"Now," Mrs. Brumpton adds, pressing the creases of both letters down. "You're probably curious to know why you're listening to all this nonsense about letters being placed in wrong envelopes." She pauses and looks into my eyes. "One of them accuses you of having a disease." She shivers.

Bruce Almighty! Birkett mixed the letters up.

I think back to being in his office, hiding behind his stinking raincoat. After Abigail interrupted him, he must have placed his mother's letter, along with the five pounds inside Mrs. Brumpton's envelope. And the letter supposed to go to Mrs. Brumpton about me, he must have placed in the envelope for his mother.

Criss-cross.

Mrs. Brumpton smiles faintly at me. "You're as healthy as a horse."

I smile faintly back.

She looks at Birkett and drops her smile. "What do you have to say for yourself?"

Birkett holds his hands out as if he's going to deny everything. He'd better not. I can run to his stinking office for his fake accounting book. I watch him carefully. He stops acting offended and for a second looks sorry. Now his face becomes an unreadable mask and he says—in a regular voice—not low, not whispering—regular, "I didn't take anything that wasn't owing to me."

"What on earth do you mean?"

"Your husband spends more on his precious cigars in one month than he does on my whole year's wages."

"What your master does and does not spend his money on has no bearing on your entitlement. In this house, it is I who employ you, and it is I you should have come to if you think you deserved more."

"You!" Birkett sneers. "Because of you, I've had to scrimp and scrape. Cutting candles in half. Weighing out sugar. You, lady, have turned me into a miser."

"Enough!" Mrs. Brumpton says. "Before you leave this house and never return, I think you owe Sally here an apology. Or shall I call a policeman?"

At the mention of the police, Birkett's eyes dart towards the door, as if the police were already standing there.

"Sally," Birkett says, using my name for the first time ever, "knows I don't need to apologize. I would never do anything to hurt her." And he looks at me with a stupid grin. "You do know that, don't you?"

They both wait for me to speak.

"Birkett," I begin, feeling a courage I've never felt before.

"Yes?" he says.

"I find that difficult to believe."

SPIRITED AWAY

A ripple of shock runs through the whole house when word gets out about Birkett. Every single servant drops what they're doing and, without arranging it, heads for the kitchen and Mrs. Meadowcroft.

Funny how good news travels so fast.

Adrian tells me that by the time Birkett had packed his suitcase, even Ma Thompson in the village had heard.

He's exaggerating.

I think.

"Did you know Birkett was on the fiddle?" Ned asks Old Jack.

Old Jack sniffs. "Hear all—see all—say nowt."

Whether that means he knew anything or not, I can't tell.

"If I was Mrs. Brumpton," Ned adds, "I'd call the constable and have him locked up."

Old Jack, looking happier than I've ever seen him; even happier than when he'd heard he was still staying to look after Copper, says, "She'd nay want the gossip, Ned Humdrum, you know that."

"Well, he's definitely out the door," Ned says.

Mrs. Meadowcroft shakes her head. "I'll believe it when I see it."

She doesn't have to wait long because we all hear Birkett slamming his office door and the sound of his footsteps marching down the passageway.

Birkett never says a word and no one speaks to him as he strides into the kitchen carrying his suitcase without wheels. The pin-dropping quiet goes on for some seconds, but as Birkett heads for the kitchen door, Old Jack speaks out. "Don't forget to SHUT THE DOOR."

I feel a rush of excitement as Adrian tugs on my sleeve and we both slip outside into the fresh air, just before Birkett does. I stand by the slop bucket . . . waiting.

Birkett glares and punches his fist at me, and I accidentally-on-purpose tip the contents of the disgusting slop bucket, covering him from head to foot in a gooey mess of molding vegetables, broken eggshells, and slimy pieces of rotten fruit.

"That's for Gerty!" I shout.

His suitcase hits the floor. It bursts open and silver teapots spill onto the gravel at his feet, and I hear Adrian gasp.

Birkett sets off running. Pieces from the slop bucket flying off his body.

Caught up in the moment, we chase after him as he darts up the path, swerves past the stables, sprints out the side gates, heads over the meadow towards the cliff path and is — gone.

SUNNY SIDE

Today, I feel like singing America the Beautiful. Everything I do from now on will be the exact opposite to what misery Birkett would have wanted.

"Maybe tomorrow we can have eggs over-easy instead of sunny-side up," I suggest to no one in particular.

"Over-easy. Sunny-side," Mrs. Meadowcroft says. "You do have a nice turn of phrase."

I smile at her. It's my day off. I'm taking it with Adrian.

"Come on," Adrian says when everyone's finished.

We gather the plates and take them through to the scullery for Gerty. She dumps them into the sink and heads out the door to join Mrs. Meadowcroft who has gone to the village for some supplies. In the kitchen, I check the stove and start adding more coal. Adrian gazes up at the April sunshine peeping through the window.

"I'll be two minutes—tops." I pitch a cloth napkin at his head.

He ducks, then play-throws the sugar tongs at me.

"Time out!" I shout, jumping out the way. They miss and fall down the dumbwaiter chute.

"Awe, no," Adrian says.

I lean over the chute. "I need a flashlight."

Adrian finds me a candle, of course, and I hold it over the chute. The sugar tongs are nowhere in sight. I try to feel for them but the floor is out of reach.

"Let me climb in," Adrian suggests.

"No way, I'm smaller." I hand him the candle.

Adrian hovers, while I hoist myself up onto the dumbwaiter ledge and swing my legs over; not easy in this long dress.

"Just don't let the dumbwaiter fall on my head," I tell him, trying to take his mind off a girl doing something he thinks he should.

I push myself off the ledge. The chute's dug a ways further than I figure, and I get a jolt when I land. Reaching down for the tongs, my hand touches something solid. But not the tongs. No. Something round and hollow. "Here, pass me that candle."

Adrian passes the candle over. "Watch your dress doesn't catch on fire," he warns.

I tilt the candle, letting the hot wax drip away from my clothes, and I shine the flame towards the floor. "It's a door. A trapdoor!"

"Can you lift it?"

I give the handle a tug with my free hand. "It's jammed." I try again. "No. I can't get it to budge."

Straightening up, I pass the candle to Adrian, and he has to help me climb back into the kitchen.

"It's definitely a trapdoor," I tell him, wiping the dust off my hands. "What d'you think it is?"

We both look at each other.

"I'll fetch a tool from Ned and lever it open," Adrian says.

"Don't waste time." I scan the kitchen and help myself to one of Mrs. Meadowcroft's meat skewers. "Use this."

Adrian climbs in and dips out of sight. "Here's the sugar tongs," he says, handing them up to me.

Next thing, he's ramming the edges of the trapdoor with the meat skewer.

Footsteps. Crunching in the yard outside.

"Stay still," I hiss. I blow the candle out. "Someone's coming."

The kitchen door bursts open and Old Jack, holding his metal tea mug from the stables, stomps over to the stove.

"Hello, Old Jack!" I shout in the direction of the dumbwaiter chute.

Old Jack lifts the teakettle and shakes it for water. "I'm not deaf, ya knows. Not yet, anyroads."

"For sure." I lean back and shield the dumbwaiter.

Old Jack makes his tea and stirs the spoon in his mug, all the time staring at me with his black eyes. I keep a stupid grin on my face. He throws the spoon down on the kitchen table, and leaves, slamming the door behind him.

I spin round in time to hear Adrian prying open the trapdoor.

"Move over!" I shout.

"No room."

"Come out, then."

"Hold on. Pass me that candle."

I light the candle again and pass it to him. "What is it?"

He bends on one knee. "The soil's sparkling!"

"What?"

"Sparkling!"

"Careful . . . what're you doing now?"

"Digging. Aye, but 'tis amazin' down here. There's this big crystal."

"Let me see." I try to look past Adrian.

"And workings."

"Workings? A machine?"

"Aye. And a tin box."

He straightens up, opens the tin box and unfolds . . . the missing page.

DISCOVERY

We take the missing page, along with Edison's drawing, to the beach below the Lifeboat House. Adrian has trouble with Edison's writing, which has flecks of rust on it from the tin box, so I read it aloud to him, stopping every now and then to stare out to sea . . .

"*'I've been in correspondence with my physicist friend and he concludes inter-dimensional travel may only be possible by distorting time.'*"

"What's a physicist?' Adrian asks.

"Dunno. We could look it up . . . how d'you look up stuff here?"

"Books."

"Oh, yeah."

I go back to Edison's page, which has faded writing in places . . .

"*'To travel through time'*—umm, something, something—*'I've found a way to harness the power of the key crystal and the tunnel of crystals below.'*"

"The key crystal must be that big one," Adrian says.

I nod. When Adrian had climbed out the dumbwaiter chute, I'd gone back in to take a look. The key crystal was the color of ice. But when I held my candle close to it, I saw shades of blue reflecting in the light.

"Keep reading," Adrian urges.

The next paragraph is about molecules. I pause to look at Adrian. He nods as if he understands what I've just read, but we spend the next ten minutes trying to figure it all out, munching on a bar of Fry's Five Boys chocolate for brain energy.

Adrian points to a side note . . .

'A handle winds the moveable axle.'

Of course, a handle. Handles wind everything in 1912.

I start to read the next bit about energy, but end up skipping most of that to get to the good stuff about the key crystal.

"*'The counter-lever connects the key crystal. After it's been energized, a series of vibrations should occur.'*"

My heart racing, I rush to the next sentence . . .

"*'I've hidden the time-travelling device in plain sight—your home's dumbwaiter, reinforced to bear the weight—but I'm concerned that a heavy and sudden movement could dislodge the counter-lever and trigger the energy flow.'*"

I clutch at Adrian's arm.

He points to the next bit . . .

As a precaution, I've added a locking device—see instructions.

I snap a piece of chocolate in two. "That lock mustn't've been on when I came down."

"Or the workmen accidentally banged it off."

"What workmen?" I ask, passing half the chocolate to Adrian.

"The day you arrived was the day we had a new rope fixed. Who knows what they fiddled with." Adrian shifts his weight on the rock we're sitting on. "Mrs. Meadowcroft told me it was the first time it'd been serviced since being built."

"When was it built?"

"I'm not sure. Before my time. She said Mr. B. had been right thoughtful back then, making the men work at night."

"Installing it at night. Sneaky." I nudge Adrian's arm. "Hey, listen to this . . . *'The instructions for setting the destination date are . . .'*"

I skip Edison's instructions. "Does that mean what I think it does?"

"I reckon you can set the date to to whatever you want."

I let out a long breath. All the tension I didn't know I was holding goes out with it to sea.

"You've nearly finished the page," Adrian points out.

I look down at Edison's writing and start reading again.

"*'The problem to solve is how to return. Must not use until we know how. Though I am tempted to live in the future.'*"

"Read that side note," Adrian urges.

"*'Tested, and for reasons I cannot fathom, fails to work. Can't ask muckers for help — top secret.'*"

I turn to Adrian. "What's muckers?"

"Happen it's his men."

"Edison thinks it doesn't work."

"Aye. Read that last bit."

"*'Too busy with money-making projects. Have locked the machine down. Works only as a dumbwaiter now.'*"

I stare out to sea.

Adrian takes Edison's drawing off me and unrolls it. "I've been at the house three years and not known about that tunnel. Other tunnels, aye. And not just me Uncle's. There's tunnels under whole of Bay. But under the dumbwaiter? No." He drops the drawing.

I pick it up.

Feeling the wonder of it all, I trace my finger over the pencil lines, letting my mind travel deep below the ground to the tunnel—sparkling and winding—connecting the house, the dumbwaiter, the future and the past.

"Penny for 'em," Adrian says, pulling my mind back up.

I fix my eyes on the horizon. "This is it, Adrian. Our chance to go back."

WHERE YOU GOING?

We head back to the house, and I can't stop planning. Adrian just listens.

For the rest of the day, I keep running to the kitchen to stare at the dumbwaiter. My fingers itching to open the trapdoor under the chute.

From our dining room, I hear Mr. Brumpton starting his car (he has to wind it at the front). I don't pay much attention until Mrs. Brumpton sends word down that he's gone to his factory, and she's closing up the house!

Maybe for good!

I stand with my mouth open.

"She's saving brass again," Mrs. Meadowcroft explains. "Their gas lamp factory's in trouble because more and more streets are switching to electric. But she says they have a friend in America who may help."

I think I can guess who.

I look over at Adrian. Thank heavens we've found the missing page. We can go to my time before the house is closed. Adrian has promised to come back with me. I can't stop talking to him about it.

The others start gossiping about Mr. Brumpton's factory, staring at the lamps as if the gas is going to stop flowing any second, and they look in no hurry to go to bed. But Adrian heads to his room. He says he needs a rest.

I don't understand. How can he sleep at a time like this?

But now Adrian's left, I don't want to stay, so I head upstairs.

Feeling the need to leave something in my room before I leave 1912, I take the hatpin out my top drawer, kneel at my usual spot, and scratch into the soft wood of the window frame . . .

Sally and Adrian

Blowing away wood slivers, I stare at my handiwork for a second, then add . . .

April 1912

* * *

Well, Adrian, maybe you can sleep, but I have to examine the key crystal and Edison's time machine again. I have to figure out how to set it. Clutching my robe with one hand, my candle lamp with the other, I open my door and make my way to our stairs.

The grandfather clock strikes twelve and the sound echoes through the sleeping house.

"Psst. Sally. Where're you going?"

I almost drop my candle lamp. Abigail is leaning over the stairs.

"Downstairs. Left something." I mouth the words in an exaggerated way so I won't have to shout.

"Don't disturb me when you come back," Abigail mouths back.

She's watching, so I head to the Brumptons' dining room, waiting to see if she'll follow. Birkett may no longer live here, but Mrs. Brumpton does.

My candle casts a long shadow on the wall. In its pale light I can just make out the dumbwaiter's box shape. I shiver against the cold, and I'm about to head for the kitchen when something on the side table catches my eye.

Tickets.

Curious, I pick one up. And what I read there makes my body freeze far more than the icy night air.

PART THREE

SHIP OF NIGHTMARES

TRAVEL PLANS

I count four tickets, then read the top one:

> WHITE STAR LINE
> First Class Passenger Ticket
> per steamship . . . Titanic
> Sailing from . . . Southampton-New York
> on . . . April 10th, 1912
> Mr. Philip Brumpton

I read the ticket again, resting my eyes on the third line: per steamship . . . *Titanic*.

Titanic!

I sift through the other tickets. Apart from Mr. Brumpton's, there's one for Mrs. Kate Brumpton, one for Lydia Brumpton, and one just marked Manservant.

No. It can't be *that* ship.

I scan the ticket again.

Yes, it says *Titanic*.

All this time they've been planning their trip to America on that doomed ship.

When?

I check the date again: April 10th, 1912.

OK. It's just turned midnight. So it's now Monday the eighth. Tuesday's the ninth. Wednesday's the tenth. That's three days.

Three days!

A cold dread grips at my stomach, and I drop the tickets on the side table and run back upstairs, wondering how come no one said. But then no one knows what's going to happen, do they?

Abigail is waiting for me outside her room. "I can't sleep," she says.

She looks at me with that fake look, and I wish I could tell her I knew she'd been Birkett's spy. But I've got more important things on my mind now.

So I force myself to be patient. 1912 people can be infuriatingly slow. "Try warm milk. It always works for my Gran."

She's about to say something else, but I dash to my room, flop down on the bed and stare through my window into the black night.

Why hadn't I remembered the *Titanic* sank in 1912? But why would I? And what do I really know about it? Apart from what I've seen on the screen. I start going over the movie in my mind. Cut out the story of Rose and Jack. Try to get to the facts.

Titanic Facts

- The *Titanic* was a brand new ship, on its maiden voyage from Southampton to New York.
- After a few days it hit a massive iceberg and went down in about two hours.
- There weren't enough lifeboats so hundreds and hundreds of passengers and crew drowned.
- The survivors were picked up by another ship; I forget its name.

So that's the plot. But it isn't a plot. It happened.

No.

It's *going* to happen.

But I've got a chance to go home. Why mess with history? They'll survive. They'll get on a lifeboat and—I get this image of Mrs. Brumpton and Lydia holding onto each other as they try to swim in ice-cold water.

I can't leave them.

But how am I going to persuade the Brumptons not to go? They know me only as a servant girl. They'd never listen. Not in a million years.

What to do? What to do?

Adrian.

Tomorrow Adrian will help. But tonight, I'll plan.

I jump out of bed, find a crumpled Ma Thompson's paper bag from my dresser drawer, and a half stub of pencil. I jump back into bed, smooth out the bag, and by the light of my candle, I write down a list of possible plans:

Plan A: Steal the tickets to prevent the Brumptons boarding the ship (wait until Abigail is out the way).

Plan B: Try to convince Mr. Brumpton the *Titanic's* unsafe. Tell him about the missing lifeboats. Appeal to his intelligence.

Plan C: Tell Mrs. Brumpton I've had a vivid dream of the *Titanic's* sinking. That my dreams always come true, so she has to listen.

But as night wears on, my ideas get more and more desperate. Plan K actually involves Adrian and me trying to push Mr. Brumpton down the dumbwaiter!

Throwing my pencil on the floor, I go kneel by my window and search the stars for answers.

None come.

I fall back into bed, exhausted. And when I sleep, I dream of home. But Orlando's dissolving and Gran's calling to me, tugging at me, telling me I should be back in the house where I belong. "Can you see home?" she calls out.

"Yes, Gran," I call back. "I can still see it."

TWO DAYS LEFT TO SAIL

My melted down candle has spilled a smooth river of wax on the nightstand. Scraps of torn-up paper bag are strewn across the floor.

Oh, yeah — the plan.

In the light of dawn, all my ideas seem pointless.

I close my eyes, hoping to get a few more precious minutes of sleep. I must have drifted off because I don't hear Gerty open my door.

"Where you going to live?" she asks, offering me a cup of tea.

I blink my eyes. "What?"

"When they close up the house. Will you go home?"

I blink again, trying to make my tired eyes open. "Gerty, I've told you before, you're not my maid. You don't have to bring me tea."

She ignores me.

"You'll miss Adrian if you go south. Mind, he won't be here, anyway, lucky thing."

"Lucky?" I mumble, rubbing my eyes.

"The biggest ship in the world. And now Adrian's going."

I sit up, fully awake. "No."

"Aye. Abigail told me. She couldn't sleep thinking about it. And about the house closing."

I love Gerty, but right now I want to strangle her. "Why is Adrian going with the family?" I ask between clenched teeth.

"Now Birkett is out, Adrian will take his place." Gerty hands me my teacup. "We're keeping it from him until Mrs. Brumpton lets him know. I can't wait to see his face." She nods her head quickly. "I'd better run. See ya downstairs."

I stare at the closed door. Birkett's gone. Now Adrian's going on the *Titanic* in his place. Me being in 1912, I've put him in danger. I've changed things. Oh, no. I've changed things. And I let the teacup fall to the floor.

* * *

Bruce Almighty! Buttons to fumble with. Apron ties to unravel. Boots to lace up. By the time I get downstairs, breakfast is over, but I've no time to eat. Time's spinning out of control and I need to take action. I can't find Adrian, so I leave an upside down spoon on the scratched table.

When I get to the stables I start pacing, making Copper restless in her stall.

Come on, Adrian. Come on.

I'm about to give up when I hear him pushing through the door.

"I thought you'd never get here," I say, trying hard not to shout.

He looks tired and his bow tie is coming undone. "I can't stay long, Mrs. Brumpton wants to see me. Where were you at breakfast?"

"I can't eat."

"Thinking about the dumbwaiter? The key crystal? Or is it Mrs. Brumpton closing up the house? Don't worry on that score, you can stay with me at Uncle Thaddeus's."

I pull strands of hair out from under my cap. "Adrian, something terrible's about to happen and I don't know what to do."

"Haven't we been through enough ginnels and come out t'other end?"

"What?"

"Ginnels is alleys."

"Look. I don't need a 1912 word lesson right now. What I need is your help."

"I'll put me Sherlock Holmes cap on."

"Get serious."

"Don't get on your high horse."

"I can't let anything happen to you, I can't. And I can't go home and—"

"Breathe, lass, breathe."

I take a deep breath. "I'm trying not to freak out, but Adrian—the Brumptons are planning to sail on the *Titanic*."

"Aye. I heard at breakfast. Amazin'."

"Adrian. The *Titanic* sinks."

"Sinks?"

"Yes sinks. And there weren't—won't be—enough lifeboats."

He shakes his head. "That's not good for the Brumptons."

"You don't know, do you?"

"Know what?"

"They're taking you with them. You're going in Birkett's place."

"I'm going America?"

"You can't go. None of you can go."

He looks disappointed. "Are you sure about the ship?"

I close my eyes. "Yes."

"So what do we do? No one listens to a maid and a footman."

I think about a couple of ideas from my plan that's still scattered in pieces on my attic bedroom floor. "We could steal the tickets. Or tell them there're not enough lifeboats. Anything to stop them getting on that ship."

"How does it sink?"

"An iceberg. It cuts a hole in the side." I sweep my hand through the air to show the hole. "The compartment thingies fill up with water—until . . ." I angle my arm downwards, my hand pointing to the floor . . . "it topples over and sinks."

I start pacing again. Copper stamps her foot. "I've thought and thought last night what to do." I stop pacing. "And we've only got today and tomorrow left. You'll be sailing Wednesday. That's just two days away."

"Two days?" Adrian frowns. "The family are leaving for Southampton docks tomorrow."

"What!"

URGENT NEWS

I race to the house, leaving Adrian to find his own way back.

"Do come in, Sally," Mrs. Brumpton calls out when she sees me hovering at the morning-room door.

"Can I speak with you, Mrs. Brumpton?"

I enter the room without waiting for her to answer.

"You're not planning on leaving us, are you, Sally? You'll wait to see if we're keeping the house? I've been very happy with your progress here and what with Gerty leaving—"

"What?"

"Please do not shout. Didn't she tell you? Oh, that's right, she's keeping it quiet for now. She's thinking of marrying the milkman. I don't know what I'll do without her. She's such a good little worker—"

I cut Mrs. Brumpton off. I can't focus on Gerty right now. "I have something very important to tell you."

"Oh?"

"It's about your trip to New York."

I move in closer to her chair and lean forward, almost touching her face.

"You must not go on the *Titanic*."

"Why ever not?"

"It's unsafe . . . it's going to sink."

URGENT NEWS

"Nonsense. Mr. Brumpton tells me that ship's been built using fine Irish craftsmanship."

Listening to Mrs. Brumpton, I feel I'm being transported right into the *Titanic* movie. She's probably going to tell me that the ship's unsinkable next.

"Yes," she says. "He read in the *Shipbuilder* that the *Titanic* is practically unsinkable."

The room spins.

"Now, Sally." Mrs. Brumpton puts on her most understanding voice. "I don't know what you've heard, but I trust Mr. Brumpton's judgment, and if he says it's safe, then, well . . ."

I wave my hands at her. "You don't understand, it's not safe. There's ice in the sea."

Mrs. Brumpton frowns.

"You have to believe me. The ship will hit an iceberg and go down quick. And there won't be enough lifeboats."

"Now, you're upset," Mrs. Brumpton begins so calmly, it makes me want to smash all her figurines into the fire. "I would like you to go to your room. Mr. Brumpton and I will be perfectly fine." Her face brightens. "Or you can do some floor scrubbing. There's a good girl. My war-on-dirt won't win itself, you know."

It's no use. She's waiting for me to leave. Her eyes follow me as I cross her rose-patterned rug.

INVISIBLE SERVANT

I don't take Mrs. Brumpton's advice. The knee-scraping floors will have to wait. But the day still disappears without a solution. Adrian suggests we go with my idea of stealing the *Titanic* tickets. But the tickets are gone from the dining room. Desperate to do something—anything—I think of Lydia.

Maybe I can convince Lydia not to go.

At this time of evening she's usually in the drawing room. I spy her through the open doorway and I wait, crouched behind a potted plant. She's reading a newspaper. Mrs. Brumpton is there with her, reading one too.

"Do you want me to wind the Edison gramophone?" Lydia asks, and my ears prick up at the sound of Edison's name.

"Not tonight," Mrs. Brumpton answers, touching her forehead as if she has a headache.

Lydia rustles her newspaper. "Look at this. I don't understand why we don't have the vote," she says. "The Isle of Man has the vote. Amusing, don't you think? An island named Man gives women the vote."

"You're going to America tomorrow," Mrs. Brumpton says, "can't you let the subject drop?" She holds out her newspaper. "Here, read this American newspaper our friend sent us."

Lydia takes the American paper and thumbs through the pages. "Listen to this, 'Isabella Goodwin gains position as the first woman detective with the New York City Police Department.' "

"Not quite a suitable position for a woman," Mrs. Brumpton points out.

"You must keep up with the times, Mother. Women are joining all sorts of professions nowadays."

Mrs. Brumpton ignores her, but Lydia interrupts again.

"Remember that fire last year? You know, the one in the Triangle shirt factory where all those girls died. Well, listen to this: 'The owners, Harris and Blanck, have received insurance monies but have yet to compensate the victims' relatives.'" Lydia turns the page over. "Then it mentions something about New York building codes, sweated labor . . ."

"Are we relaxing or not?" Mrs. Brumpton interrupts, touching her head again.

"No, no, listen," Lydia insists. "'An inspection of their new factory premises exposed Harris and Blanck of again breaking the law—locked doors and piles of material on the floors were found.'"

"Really, Lydia," Mrs. Brumpton says. "Do stop reading gloomy stories about New York or you're not going to enjoy your trip."

"Gloomy! Those girls died, and for what?" Lydia glares at her father's chair. "So greedy factory owners can make a profit."

"You know nothing about it. Your father . . ."

But Lydia doesn't wait to hear the rest. She tosses the newspaper on the floor and storms out. I move away from the potted plant, but she rushes past and up the stairs. She doesn't even notice me. I sprint up after her and knock on her bedroom door.

The door opens a crack. "Yes, Sally?"

"Can I come in, Lydia?"

She arches an eyebrow but lets me in. I'm breaking 1912 rules again.

"I saw you running up the stairs. You all right?"

"I'm quite well, thank you." Lydia sits on her bed and starts braiding her hair. I'm distracted for a second, looking at her hair the same color as mine.

"Oh, who am I fooling?" Lydia blurts out. "I try to pretend everything's perfectly splendid; try to be the good girl Mother wants me to be. I don't even understand it myself."

I turn and face her. "But you can leave if you want."

Just don't go on the Titanic.

"I can't just up and go on my own."

"I did." It wasn't an accusation. I could hear the hurt in my voice.

"Your class can."

Class? Does she mean from school? I ignore it. "In the future things will be better."

Lydia undoes her newly braided hair and begins braiding it again. "You mean, I'll find a nice young man and settle down."

"Why settle down when there's a whole world to see?"

Just not America, yet.

"You make it sound so easy."

I start straightening her clothes near her travel trunk and try to think of something dramatic to say to give her hope. "One day women will change the world."

Lydia stops braiding. "You'd make a good suffragette."

I fold one of her corsets. "What does a suffragette do, anyway?"

"Do? Drastic action to get men to listen."

"Like what?"

"Don't you read the paper?"

I hesitate.

"Sorry," Lydia says. "You probably don't have the time. Well, they chain themselves to railings, go on hunger strikes—whatever it takes. I wish I had their courage but I don't want to go to prison."

"Does suffragette mean to suffer, then?"

A trace of a smile crosses Lydia's lips. "It means to fight for suffrage—the right to vote." She looks in her dresser mirror. I know she's not seeing herself in there. "We could change things if we got the vote."

"America lets women vote, right?"

Lydia shakes her head. "Sally, sometimes you sound so grown-up; sometimes so young."

Time travel will do that to you, I want to tell her. Instead, I say, "Well, you know, America, land of the free. I just thought we—they—would have."

"There are a couple of places in America." Lydia stands up. "And the world hasn't come to an end in them." She moves to the door and holds it open. "Which reminds me, young lady, I have a trip tomorrow."

Just for a second, I'd forgotten. "Don't go," I beg. "Don't go tomorrow."

"I thought you said the whole world was waiting for me."

"Yes, but . . ." I stumble on my thoughts. "That ship's not safe."

"Now, really."

"I mean it. Don't go. You . . . you could begin your fight for votes here. In Robin Hood's Bay."

Lydia smiles. "In Robin Hood's Bay? Haven't you noticed, Sally? Nothing ever happens here."

STRESSED

Our dining room is deserted. The gas turned low. But there's an upside down spoon on the scratched table. I run to the stables, trying not to trip over anything in the dark. Adrian's standing just inside. His lantern is on the floor and the burning light makes him look ghostly.

"Did Lydia listen?' he asks, as I try to get back my breath.

"No. And now she's upset."

"About the *Titanic?*"

I shake my head. "Something she read in the newspaper."

I pause for a second to think. If only I could find someone to persuade Mrs. Brumpton. Someone she respected. But no one in 1912 suspects a thing. This isn't just an immigrant ship. It's a luxury liner. The best of the red-carpet best. Nothing could possibly go wrong. And nothing could persuade her not to go.

But what if their trip were cancelled? What if they *had* to choose another place to go?

I grab Adrian's arm. "Go into the house and sneak out the Sunday paper for me."

He hesitates.

"Just watch out for Abigail."

Adrian's gone so long bringing me the newspaper, I'm convinced Abigail's figured out our secret code.

"About time," I snap, when Adrian finally pushes through the stable door.

"I had to wait for Mrs. Brumpton to leave the drawing room."

Adrian spreads the newspaper over a hay bale and holds his lantern over our heads for light. Running my finger down each page, I pore over the black-and-white advertisements. I find trips to seaside towns such as Brighton and Clacton-on-Sea. Cycling tours seem popular in these places. But I can't imagine Mrs. Brumpton on a bike.

"We need a trip to somewhere different," I tell him. "They already live in a seaside town. Here's one, this looks promising."

THE SS *NOMADIC*, STEADIEST SHIP TO HOLLAND. COME SEE THE TULIPS, NOW IN BLOOM. BOOKING OFFICE, 47B PIER ROAD, WHITBY.

"Aye, but you'll never get to see Mrs. Brumpton tonight," Adrian says. "And we're supposed to be off first thing."

"Is there a public callbox? I haven't seen one in the village."

Adrian combs his fingers through his curls. "Callbox?"

"I don't know. Place for a phone." I throw my cap on the floor. "Why do I have to explain everything?"

"The only telephone is at the Robin Hood Inn. The guests use it. 'Tis in an alcove at the foot of the stairs. You could sneak in the side door. But you won't get to make a call tonight."

"Why not?"

"The landlord locks it up after dark."

Bruce Almighty! The telephone is the only modern technology in this village and now I can't even use that.

No, I'm wrong. There is another technology in the village.

"There's a train station, right?"

"Aye, but—"

"Tomorrow I'm going to try to convince Mrs. Brumpton that her tickets are cancelled." I fold the newspaper. "But if that doesn't work, I'll find Mr. Brumpton at his factory and tell him Edison's dumbwaiter worked. That I'm from the future. So he needs to listen."

Adrian stares at me for a second. "You're not going to the factory alone."

I'm about to say stop being so 1912, but change my mind. "Then pretend you're going to Southampton docks alone, and come with me too."

ONE DAY LEFT TO SAIL

This morning there's a buzz going around our scratched dining table about Adrian going to America. But he's not here. Where *is* he? It's not like him to miss breakfast. I try all the usual places in the house he could be: our stairs, the kitchen, the dining room, the lamp room, the scullery, even his room.

No luck.

If I'm going to telephone Mrs. Brumpton in the village, I need to go—now.

So, after it's cleared, I leave a knife on our dining table, pointing towards the door, and I head to the donkey path.

* * *

The Robin Hood Inn, its windows blinking in the early morning sun, looks deserted. The side door's open. Good. And the phone's on the wall in a little alcove at the foot of the stairs, just the way Adrian described last night.

The sign above the phone reads: *Telephone Calls—Three Pennies Each*. And on a shelf there's a tin can with a slit in the top. I drop a couple of threepenny coins into the tin can, and pull out a script I wrote last night.

The phone has no buttons to push, just an earpiece to hold, a speaker to talk into, and a winding handle. I pick up the earpiece and wind the handle. Someone taps me on the shoulder, and I drop the earpiece. I can hear the operator saying, "Hello, hello," as the earpiece swings on its cord.

"Adrian!"

"Quick!" he says. "Mrs. Brumpton and Lydia are leaving soon. They want me to catch the train now. I made an excuse and told them I'm catching the next one."

"Good 'cos there's no way you're boarding that ship. Now let me try this." I pick up the earpiece. "Hello. Operator. Could you dial Brumpton Manor for me?"

"One minute; I'll connect you," the operator says.

I stare at the speaker. *Don't let Abigail answer. Don't let Abigail answer.*

"Good morning, Brumpton Manor," Abigail answers. I slam down the earpiece.

"Let's go," Adrian urges.

"No. One more time."

I ask the operator to connect me, and I hover with the earpiece in my hand, ready to slam it down in case Abigail answers again.

"Kate Brumpton of Brumpton Manor."

Phew. But Mrs. Brumpton's voice sounds as if it were coming from the far corner of the planet instead of just five minutes at the end of the donkey path.

"This is the White Star Line," I begin, reading from my script and trying to disguise my voice with an English accent. "I'm calling to say that there's been a mix-up with your reservations."

Adrian stares at me in amazement.

There's a crackling sound on the line, and Mrs. Brumpton says, "Who is this? Let me talk to the man in charge."

I drop my script. Adrian scoops it up and hands it back.

"I am in charge," I answer, forgetting to use my fake

English voice. I go back to the script and try again. "We can offer you another first-class trip to Holland. The tulips are in full bloom this time of year and you'll have a panoramic view—"

Click. The phone goes dead. I wind the handle again. Adrian tugs at my arm.

"Hell-o," the operator says.

"I was cut off from my call to Brumpton Manor," I tell her. "Could you put me through again?"

"One moment, please."

I wait with the earpiece pressed to my ear. In the background I can hear the operator saying: "I'm looking up that number for you, Mrs. Brumpton. Is White Star one word or two?"

I crumple up my script. Now Mrs. Brumpton's on the phone calling the White Star Line, and she'll find her reservations on the *Titanic* are just fine.

"Come on," Adrian begs.

I slam the earpiece back on its hook.

It was a stupid idea anyhow.

FOR YOUR EYES ONLY

Back at the house there's nothing we can do. Mrs. Brumpton and Lydia are upstairs getting ready, and Abigail won't let me anywhere near them. Everyone else is far too busy to notice Adrian and me creep out the scullery door. Apart from Smudge that is, standing by an upstairs window.

But there's Ned in the backyard, smoking a cigarette and leaning on his rake.

We double back and duck behind the scullery wall, James Bond style.

I shift positions and the damp brick scrapes my back. Adrian is hiding the address of Mr. Brumpton's factory in his pocket. I don't like the idea of telling Mr. Brumpton the time-travel truth. What if he tells the whole world? What if he pulls apart the dumbwaiter? But I can't see my way round it.

Adrian peeps over the wall and gives me a sign that Ned's still there. I check the scullery door. Mrs. Meadowcroft will be locking it up soon. Locking up my chance to go back.

Adrian looks over the wall again, and this time signs the way's clear.

We make a dash for the gate, yelling all the way. So much for keeping quiet. I don't think 007 will have any competition from us.

We head for Uncle Thaddeus's empty cottage along lanes I haven't been on before. Adrian says it's the back way to the station as well as a shortcut. We're going to the cottage through the beach tunnel, which is another back way, another shortcut, away from prying eyes.

At the beach the tide is out enough for us to step to the tunnel without getting feet wet. Adrian has left a lantern in a rock crevice just inside the opening. He lights it, and when we get to the top of the steps, I can now see that the prickly rock is made of crystal. The same kind that's under the dumbwaiter; the same as the key crystal. I push the thought away of going back home, as Adrian pushes open the trapdoor.

* * *

I shiver in Uncle Thaddeus's unheated cottage.

There are coins on the table and a cardboard box. After placing his lantern down, Adrian scoops up the box, hands it to me and says, "Here, I never want you to be cold again."

Forgetting everything for a moment, I open it up. Wrapped in tissue paper is a new coat! A gorgeous deep green one. I hold it up. There are seven buttons down the front that fasten onto soft velvet loops.

So that's where he was earlier: Shopping!

It fits perfect.

"There's more," he says.

In the layers of tissue paper, I find a matching hat and a hatpin like the one in my top drawer.

"Why but it looks grand next to your hair," Adrian says, nodding towards my coat.

I feel my face blush.

"Help me put the hat on," I say to distract him. "I've never used a hatpin before."

He takes the hat and secures it. For once I'm having a

good hair day and it doesn't tumble down my back at the slightest touch.

I hug the warm coat around me and press one of the soft velvet loops. "Thank you."

Now it's his turn to blush.

"You shouldn't have spent your pay on me," I tell him.

Adrian fiddles with the coins on the table. "I'll take it back, then?"

"Never."

THE TRAIN

The train station is empty except for a uniformed ticket man busy weeding around daffodils in a triangle of soil near the fence. When he sees us, he stretches up, and washes his hands at the outside faucet before heading to his ticket office. I peer through his open window. A comfy chair is pushed next to a stove. The air smells of coffee. Of home. I'm about to change my mind about going when Adrian asks for return tickets.

The ticket man leans his elbow on the counter. "You two young 'uns goin' on a trip?"

"We're doing some business for the master," Adrian says, as he searches his pockets for the ticket money. He pulls out a book, a paper bag (bulging with something square and flat), his *Titanic* ticket, and his lucky heart-shaped coin.

My heart quickens at the sight of his *Titanic* ticket.

Adrian hides it from the ticket man's eyes, as he pulls out a handful of coins. "I must've left the rest of my money at Uncle Thaddeus's."

And I remember the coins he was fiddling with on the table.

The ticket man shrugs. "No brass—no ticket." And he turns to fill his coffee mug.

I pull Adrian away from the ticket window and check my uniform dress pocket. I find a few coins.

Adrian shakes his head. "Not enough for a return trip."

"Credit card?" He is earning. He could have one.

"What?"

"No plastic of any kind?"

"What's plastic?"

I tug at the sleeve of my lovely new coat. "Shall I take my coat back to the store?"

Adrian turns to the ticket man's window, taps on the glass and asks for two one-way tickets.

* * *

A blast of steam, so loud I have to cover my ears, signals our train's arrival on Platform B.

"All 'board!" the ticket man cries.

Adrian opens the train door for me, and holds out his hand to help me board. I ignore it, of course. I'm perfectly capable of stepping onto a train.

We have a private car, or compartment as Adrian calls it, all to ourselves. Hogwarts Express style. Adrian lowers the window and sticks his head out. The ticket man blows his whistle and waves his little flag, and the train huffs and puffs out the station.

Phew! We've actually made it.

There are two comfy looking red bench seats opposite each other. On one compartment wall is a framed picture of the seaside. I kneel on one of the seats and check it out. A sign underneath says *Enjoy Sunny Scarborough*. Two ladies wearing frilly caps and knee-length, lace-trimmed swimming outfits, are smiling down at me. I can't see how anyone could enjoy sunny anywhere in such a get-up. Why, even their legs are covered in the thick black stockings I've given up on wearing.

THE TRAIN

I turn round, settle on the bench seat and unfasten the velvet hoops of my new coat.

Adrian pulls his head back in and closes the window. "We're in for a long ride," he says, patting his wind-blown curls down.

"How far is it to Mr. Brumpton's factory?"

He takes out his golden watch and opens it. "Not sure." He clicks the lid shut.

"What time will we get there?"

Adrian flips open the lid of his watch again. "Don't know." He snaps it shut and gives it a polish. "But 'tis a long way," he says, and I realize he doesn't have a clue about travelling outside Yorkshire.

I turn my attention to the countryside view outside the window. The train curves round the track and the coastline appears. The sun throws diamonds on the sea. I think of Gerty getting married soon. Even as I ask myself the question: Does she want to marry the milkman just to get away from her job? I know the answer.

Yes.

I peel off my new coat and rest it carefully on the hammock-style luggage rack above. The train gathers speed. It makes a comforting sound as it travels smoothly over the metal tracks: du-du-du-da, du-du-du-da, du-du-du-da.

We pass through Whitby where an abbey rises high on a hill. And Scarborough where the top of the Grand Hotel's corner turrets look like huge upside-down cups.

Adrian startles me by sliding open our door to the train's corridor. A wonderful whiff of cooked food floats down from what must be the dining area, making my mouth water. Adrian eyes both ends of the passage, then closes the door. "No man to punch our ticket yet."

"Or woman," I say, and he half smiles.

To take my mind off my hunger—and if I'm hungry, Adrian's starving—we chat about the other servants and where they're going to live, and what their reaction must be at finding us gone. Then, lost in our own thoughts, we settle back for the long ride and stare at the sea.

Tomorrow the *Titanic* will sail. My stomach turns over at the thought.

If only that iceberg hadn't formed and floated into the Atlantic. If only there'd been enough lifeboats. If only . . . but then the *Titanic* was full of *if-only*s. And now we're on this train trying to do what? Stop one family. What about all the other families on their way to New York? How do we stop them?

"The ship of dreams," I blurt out.

"What?" Adrian says.

"That's what they called the *Titanic*. The ship of dreams."

"If only they knew."

Yeah, I think, closing my eyes.

If only.

GET OFF THE TRAIN

We fall asleep in the gently rocking train and are awoken rudely by a porter telling us to get off, it's the end of the line.

Adrian helps me fix my hat.

"Shall we see if there's a tram or an omnibus to the factory?" he asks, as we step off the train.

"A what or a what?"

"Transport."

"OK," I say, staring longingly at the Cadbury's chocolate bars lined up on the snack stand behind him.

We exit the station, and the stale smelling air hits me as we set off up a hill in the same direction as everyone else. We're jammed between a group of girls carrying baskets. They don't seem to mind touching our elbows; I can feel the rough wool of one girl's shawl and the bump of her basket. She looks up with interested eyes at Adrian.

He doesn't notice.

Feeling lucky to have Adrian all to myself, away from the house and his job that keeps us apart so much, I gaze down at the town below. To our right is street after street of row houses. To our left is a murky brown river snaking its way along the edge of a brick building.

"I think that's the factory." Adrian points down. "We can walk to it."

We make our way towards the river, and as we get nearer, I notice the factory windows are blackened with dirt. BRUMPTON LAMPS, the name on the bricks says, and my stomach knots in a tight twist at the thought of telling Mr. Brumpton what year I'm really from.

At the open gates, Adrian insists on going into the factory to check where Mr. Brumpton is, and before I can stop him, he runs inside.

While I'm waiting, an ear-splitting whistle blows, and a sea of men, women and children all come clomping out. I have to dart to one side so I won't be crushed. The noise of their footwear on the road is deafening. The men look hard and the women look worn out, but the children are laughing and pushing each other as if they're just been let out of school.

Adrian appears out of the crowd and tells me Mr. Brumpton's gone.

"What do you mean, gone?"

"To Southampton docks. He's met the family off the train and is taking them there."

I try to take it in. "Do we have enough money for a ticket to the docks?"

"I don't rightly know."

The light's fading and not sure of what to do, we leave the factory and stop on the opposite side of the road, outside a rundown store. A tight-lipped woman inside is locking-up and pulling down the door blind. She gives me a mean stare, and I suddenly long with all my heart to jump on the next train back to Robin Hood's Bay. I don't tell Adrian, who's busy counting coins under an unlit streetlight.

The factory people have left. The town's quiet now, and it gives me the creeps. Just when I'm thinking there's not one person left in the whole world, a man trots towards us, carrying a ladder. He leans his ladder against the streetlight, climbs it, touches the light with something in his hand, and a weak glow spills onto the road.

Adrian peers up from his coin counting and touches his cap. "Evenin', yon lamplighter."

"Evenin', sonny," the lamplighter says. He climbs down, tucks his ladder under his arm and sprints off.

These must be the lamps Mr. Brumpton makes. Soon to be replaced with electric. That's why he's going to see Thomas Edison in America. I know Edison had something to do with inventing electric light bulbs. He probably has some good advice. Funny, though, Robin Hood's Bay doesn't have any streetlights. Except for the moon and the stars.

"How much money do we have?" I ask Adrian, impatient with his coin counting.

"Tuppence short of two shillings."

A rumbling sound disturbs the quiet street. "By the way," Adrian says. "*That* is a tram."

"Oh, a streetcar." The streetcar rattles and sways on its tracks and comes to a stop. "Do we have enough for a ticket?"

Adrian shakes his head. "It'll be local, anyroad."

"Too bad."

The streetcar moves off, and I push away the desire to jump on.

Adrian starts hunting his pockets for coins again. He pulls out the bulky paper bag I saw when he emptied his pockets out at Bay's train station, and passes it to me to hold.

"I meant to show you those," he says. "They're some of the photographs Lydia took. She gave me them."

This is no time for photographs.

I tuck them in my coat pocket without so much as a flip through.

Something catches my eye. In the shadows, standing in the store doorway opposite, is a man wearing an immaculate black suit. He wasn't there a minute ago, so he must have got off the tram. He stares at us as he lights a cigarette. He's the smartest looking man I've ever seen in 1912. I notice too, his hat is a black top hat. It makes him look like he belongs in one of my black-and-white movies. Like Fred Astaire in *Top Hat*.

He tosses his match to the ground and crosses the road. "'Scuse me," he says to Adrian, though he gives my new green coat a polite nod. "Couldn't help noticing you look lost. Can I help?"

"We're lookin' for a ride to Southampton," Adrian answers.

"Come with me, young man," he says, his black hat shimmering in the lamplight. "I'll see what I can do."

I can't take my eyes off his smart suit, but for the first time, I notice a tiny hole in the knee.

He gives Adrian a man-to-man look. "You don't want the little lady walking round here at night."

I have a sixth sense we should run the other way, but I ignore it and follow Adrian and the top hat through the streets. He takes us to the front of a hotel with an impressive set of double doors, even if the paint is peeling.

"Here we are. Now you give me your coins, and I'll make sure you get a safe ride from a friend of mine that stays in this here fine establishment."

One of the doors opens, and a group of men fall out. They lift their collars up, push past, and head off into the gaslit street. I get a glimpse inside of a smoke-filled room and men silently drinking. Adrian hands over our coins to the top hat, and he disappears into the hotel. We move to the other side of the street and watch the doors.

We wait and wait.

And wait.

Finally, Adrian realizes we've been duped. "Probably did a runner out back."

I step into the road onto the tram tracks and face Adrian with both hands on my hips. I'm hungry, tired, scared. You name it, I'm feeling it. "What did you give him our money for?" I hurl the words at him across the street.

He staggers back. "What?"

"You heard me. What idiot hands over his money to a

person they've never met before? Haven't you heard of stranger danger or—" I stop. Adrian's expression is the worst mixture of hurt and shock I've ever seen.

"You know what, clever clogs?" he shouts, and I immediately forget his hurt expression. "If you hadn't thought to traipse us all over yon country we wouldn't be in this mess, so why don't *you* get us to Southampton or, better yet, take us home where I can be warm and fed and don't have to mither about strangers." And he storms off.

"Wait up!" Something about seeing him walk away like that really freaks me out. "Adrian!" I shout up the street. "Please stop."

I go after him. I have to take little runs to keep up. He turns a corner. But when I reach the corner, he's gone.

What have I done? I've no money. No clue where I am. And no idea of what to do. I run towards the only store with its light reflecting into the street. Is Adrian in there? He has to be. I peer through the window. A stooping man is behind the counter, locking away a tray of rings.

Adrian is standing opposite.

I bang on the window, and they both turn to see. Adrian waves me in.

Inside the store there are racks of men's suits and shelves with dust-covered clocks and stuff to do with horses; even half a statue of a horse.

"How much?" Adrian asks, holding out his pocket watch.

I hadn't expected this. Not a pawn store. How can he think of parting with his precious watch?

The stooped man holds Adrian's watch up to his ear and shakes it. The tips of his fingers are stained with yellow. "Five bob," he offers.

"Five shillings!" Adrian shouts. "Just look at the engraving."

The stooped man opens Adrian's watch and studies the engraving of the ship. "All right, six shillings."

Adrian holds out his hand. "I think I saw another pawn shop near the station."

"I tell you what," the stooped man says. "Seven shillings; not a penny-farthing more."

I shake my head. This place may not be anything like the pawn store Gran goes to on Seven Dwarfs Lane, but it's still the same idea. People pawning their possessions for next to nothing. It makes me sad. Not to mention Gran never has the money to get her stuff back.

"Don't do it," I whisper in Adrian's ear.

"Seven shillings and I'll throw in a new chain when you pick it up," the stooped man offers.

Adrian takes his watch back, and we edge our way past the horse statue, towards the door.

"Please yourself," the stooped man calls after us.

Outside, I stand at the doorway, waiting. Will Adrian remember our fight?

"Pop quiz," Adrian says after a moment. "What if I gets us out of here. Would that suit your ladyship?"

"No," I say softly. "How about we *both* get us out of here?"

And he smiles his smile, and the town fades away.

FRUSTRATION

We tramp through the dismal streets, looking for inspiration. We've no train tickets. No money for a meal. No chance of getting to Southampton on time. I want to say I wish there were cash machines, but I know I'd be wasting my breath. If only I'd saved some of my pay, but the money here just doesn't feel like real money. I push my hands in my empty pockets. Well, it feels real now. Now that I've none.

"'Tis no good," Adrian moans. "We'll have to go back."

Of course when we re-enter the pawn store, the old pawnbroker gives us a smug look. "I'll give you five-and-six, seein' as you're in such a fix."

Adrian shakes his head. "'Tis your offer of seven shillings, or I'm walking."

"'Tis a nice piece," the pawnbroker admits, "but I've dozens like it, so six shillings and that's me last offer. Takes it or leaves it."

Adrian looks down at the dusty floor. The seconds tick by. He looks back up at the pawnbroker, but the old man's eyes remain hard. Adrian unthreads his watch, the only link left to his drowned dad, and he passes it over.

"And the chain," the pawnbroker insists with a stare that says, I won't settle for less.

Adrian slowly drops the chain into the pawnbroker's stained hand.

I look away.

* * *

Outside, Adrian pockets his shilling coins.

"Let's eat," I suggest. Though my appetite's gone, anything to get that pawn-store look off Adrian's face.

"How about fish-and-chips?" he says. "I saw a place near the station."

We make our way back, and pick up fish-and-chips to go, wrapped in newspaper. Adrian has vinegar on his fries.

Twenty minutes later, I ignore Adrian's helping hand again as we board the train.

Pulling my green coat off, I gaze with relief at the room-like compartment. Two lighted lamps now protect us from the black night outside. With a jolt the train sets off and we leave behind the smoke and the dirt and the town I never want to see again.

What would Gran say if she knew I'd been roaming the streets after dark? I know Dad would have gone nuts. Grounded me for weeks. I wish he was here to do that now.

I glance over at Adrian. In the train's soothing rhythm he's fallen asleep, one hand over the pocket where his watch used to be. I force myself to stay awake. We're on a mission. We mustn't miss our stop. We mustn't miss the *Titanic*.

NOT THERE YET

The lights flicker and the train comes to a stuttering halt, just before the station.

"No," Adrian groans.

"Problem on the line," a porter with a mustache tells us. "You can either get out here or stay on till the line's fixed—it's up to you."

"When's the next train?" I ask.

"You've just missed the nine-fifteen," he tells us, glancing up towards the station clock. "Next one going that way is the ten-twenty."

"Thanks," Adrian says.

The porter's mustache twitches. "Tomorrow."

"Tomorrow!" I shout. "That's too late."

We hear the sound of heavy doors slamming, and I stand to leave but change my mind and flop back down.

What's the use?

I throw my hat on the seat opposite. Nothing matters now.

The train blows steam from its engines. I lean my head against the window and watch as three railroad men swing pickaxes by lamplight, on the far side.

Adrian's waiting for me to tell him what to do. I don't

care because in my mind the Brumptons are standing on the *Titanic*'s deck. I can see their faces through the steam. Ghostly portraits hanging in the air.

Half-heartedly, I pull Lydia's photographs from my pocket and sift through them. They're not that good. Most of them are nearly all sky or out of focus. But there's Adrian next to the water pump outside Ma Thompson's. And here I am, standing in front of the bicycle shop with my hair blowing in the breeze. Though no one would know it was me. My face is all smudgy. Lydia must have put her finger over the lens.

Hang on. I've seen this picture before.

But the world must be playing tricks because that's not possible.

And now I see it. The crumpled photograph of a girl in front of a bicycle shop; the shadowy imprint of someone's finger; Gran's pale, shocked stare . . . I spring out of my seat. "I remember. I remember where I've seen the Brumptons before."

"Where?" Adrian asks, pulling himself up straight.

"In old photographs. Gran was always trying to show me old family photos but I never took any notice. And look, this photograph is of me. Me! And my aunt has it now. Do you hear me? My aunt has this photograph."

"How can your aunt have a photograph of you taken in 1912? It makes no sense."

I sit back down. "None of this makes sense, does it? Falling down a dumbwaiter that's a time machine, and the next thing you know I'm here in 1912 working as a maid, pretending I'm in a movie, taking it moment by moment and . . . and I knew I was a Brumpton. Deep down, I felt it."

"A Brumpton, aye? Does that mean I have to take me cap off every time I see you?"

"You'd better."

He pulls his cap off. "M'lady."

I'm about to bow my head but change my mind. I feel serious again. The Brumptons are my family. Does that mean they survived without my help? Or—or did only Lydia make it off the *Titanic*. Oh, I wish I'd listened more to Gran and her stories about the past.

"Look," Adrian says, putting his cap on. "Let's get off this train, Sally Soforth or Sally Brumpton or whatever your name is. Maybe we can get to Southampton by another route."

Adrian checks at the station, and sure enough, if we buy a ticket to Waterloo and change trains, we can reach Southampton by morning. It's amazing what some cash thrown at the problem can do.

Twenty minutes later, Adrian's offering his hand out to help me board a train again. I ignore it and jump on.

NO MORE DAYS LEFT

We hurry through the streets of Southampton, alongside rows of hotels and stores with striped canopies. Box-shaped cars are lined up down the high street, next to horses and carriages. Electric trams rumble past. We dodge our way across the busy street. The clip clop noise of horses' hooves mixed with the whirr of car engines and honking horns makes Adrian cover his ears. I'm thinking it's the type of town I'd like to stop and explore if we had the time.

But time is running out.

At last we reach the entranceway to the docks. A policeman is standing at the gates. He looks hot and unhappy in his high-necked uniform.

Adrian touches his cap. "Which way to the *Titanic?*"

"Berth 44," the policeman answers in an I've-been-saying-this-all-morning tone.

"What time is it?" I ask.

Adrian reaches for his watch, then pulls his empty hand away.

The policeman checks his own pocket watch.

"Eleven-forty-five," he says. "Dead on."

"Has the *Titanic* sailed yet?" We both ask at the same time.

"Let me just look in me crystal ball." The policeman cups his hands, pretending to hold a ball. "Nope. Must be foggy at Berth 44, can't see a thing."

We leave him grinning at his own joke, and set off running. I undo my coat loops. Adrian looks back to see if I'm keeping up.

Were we too late?

The question hangs in the sea air as we sprint through the docks, racing past huge sheds filled with barrels, past workshops busy with dockworkers, past other berths and other ships until at last we reach the dock where Berth 44 is. And there she is. Her new paint gleaming.

Titanic.

Smoke is rising from her funnels, swirling round the top of a crane. On every side people are waving—white hankies, straw hats, little flags—holding up babies and squirming toddlers. I count, one, two, three . . . six tugboats in the water, all toy-sized under the shadow of the ship, though we can hear their engines thumping, see their smoke billowing. We make our way towards the quayside. The crowd presses in, and Adrian takes my hand.

His hand keeps me from shaking, but I'm frightened the ship will start moving. "Do something, Adrian."

Adrian calls up a gangplank, "Let us on, mister."

"Too late," the seaman shouts back. "Try first-class."

We edge alongside the ship, pushing through the crowd. "Watch it, ducks!" someone shouts. "Learn some manners, young lady," another calls.

I take no notice. I'm scanning the ship's railings, desperately searching for any sign of the Brumptons. But it's no use. Every woman's face is Mrs. Brumpton's, every cigar-smoking man is Mr. Brumpton, every fine hat is Lydia's.

The first-class gangplank hasn't been closed yet. My heart thumps as I fasten up the loops of my coat, rehearsing in my head what I'm about to say to the Brumptons. I've decided to invent a story about an emergency at the house. I thought it could be a fire. Not a burned-to-the-ground fire. Just the chimney, perhaps. Or a section of the roof. Enough to get them home.

Halfway up the gangplank, we do a double take at a cat coming towards us. She's carrying two kittens in her mouth. We sidestep the cat, and she pads to the bottom and leaves the ship.

Wise cat.

An important looking seaman holds up his hand. "Hey, hey, now. Where're you two going? This ship's about to sail."

"Yes," I answer, trying to act confident. "We just made it. Our train was delayed."

"Let's see your tickets."

"Tickets? No, I need to speak to the Brumptons. It's an emergency."

"They'll be on this passenger list, then," he says, tapping the clipboard in his hand.

I move in closer as he flips through a couple of pages. "Yes, that's them—Brumpton, Mr. Philip and Mrs. Kate." I point to Lydia's name underneath. "And their daughter—Lydia. Lydia Brumpton."

"What's your name?"

"Sally Soforth." I adjust my hat. "I'm a family friend."

The seaman nods towards Adrian. "And who's he?"

I remember what's written on Adrian's ticket. "This is their manservant, their butler." I give Adrian a promotion to make him sound more important.

The seaman weighs Adrian up and down. "A bit young for a butler, isn't he?"

"He's older than he looks."

"Stewardess," the seaman calls over his shoulder to a striking, slim lady juggling bunches of flowers in her arms.

"Go to state room number" he glances down at his list "B-33. And bring Mr. Brumpton here."

"Yes, sir," she answers, the flowers framing her pretty face.

I sense Adrian breathing behind me. I shield him from the ship. The seaman stares at me, and I realize he's not going to move. I avoid his stare and look down at my right foot. It feels different. The ship's vibrating through my boot.

I'm actually standing on the *Titanic!*

The telephone rings, and the seaman snatches it up. "Lightholler." He listens without taking his eyes off me. Something's wrong. I can tell by his eyes. So can Adrian because he shows the seaman his ticket.

"No, Adrian," I snap. "You're not getting on."

"Someone's got to help them."

"No!"

The ship's horn blasts.

What happens next is fast. Adrian is separated from me and pulled onto the *Titanic*. The seaman pushes me back. But I want to reach Adrian. I move forward and, without saying a word, he passes me all the coins in his pocket. I try to grab his hand and pull him off the ship, but the seaman pulls him away. Tears prick my eyes. The seaman says I must go. Now.

"Get them in the lifeboats," I call as another seaman appears and pulls me down the gangplank. I look back. The seaman called Lightholler is staring at me with a puzzled expression. Adrian looks lost, hanging over the railings. I'm now in the crowd and I can't believe he's up there, on board the *Titanic*. The horn blasts again and the tiny tugboats start nudging the huge ship away from the dockside.

I snap out of my daze and try to keep up as the *Titanic* glides downstream. I hold my hand up to the ship and hope Adrian can see me.

I trip on my bootlace and have to kneel to fix it, and when

I look up, the *Titanic*'s in trouble. It's trying to squeeze its way past a another ship tied up in the dock, and this ship is pulling towards the *Titanic* like a magnet, edging closer and closer.

Bang!

The metal ropes on the other ship have snapped, and I watch the sky with my mouth open as one flips backwards into the sea. The two ships are now dangerously close. Adrian's out there, and I've no clue what's going on. Have I changed things again by being here? Then I realize. If the *Titanic* is damaged in a collision, it won't be able to sail. The best thing that can happen right now is that this loose ship out there hits the *Titanic,* just hard enough to stop the bigger disaster.

But at the last possible second, the *Titanic* pulls back, and one of the tugs in the water starts nudging the other ship away. I sigh. There's going to be no change in history this time.

"That wasn't in the movie," I say aloud.

And for once, it doesn't feel like my movie. The noise, the dock, the ships. Everything's so real.

The *Titanic* has now stopped. Delayed. I wait, hoping something else will happen to make it turn back, but it starts to move again.

I watch the passengers pressed against the railings, waving to the crowd. They look too happy. They look too relaxed. A mother in the crowd holds up her chubby baby and kisses its cheek, "Wave to Daddy," the mother says, and I feel the terrible burden of knowing the future.

Stop! Stop! I want to shout. Don't you know? You're doomed.

The ship answers me with a haunting, shuddering blast of its horn.

Trembling, I turn away.

MESSAGES

Adrian. Adrian. How could I have left you on that ship?

I stumble through the docks, not caring if the crowd jostles me or not. What's wrong with me? In a few days that iceberg will hit. If only I could talk to a friendly voice. See a friendly face in the crowd. If only Mrs. Meadowcroft were here.

I have to phone her.

A hotel. I need a hotel.

I'm nearly at the dock gates. The policeman's still there, eyeing the crowds now leaving. I tell him I want a hotel, and he directs me to one called The Dolphin.

* * *

The doorman opens the door for me.

First, I go splash my face in the washroom and dry my hands on one of the rolled-up hand towels. Then I straighten my hat. Thanks to my new coat, I don't look out of place. The hotel clerk in the lobby is extra kind when I ask her for the telephone. "What a fetching hat," she says.

Abigail answers the phone. But I'm ready for her and pretend I'm a relation of Mrs. Meadowcroft's.

Mrs. Meadowcroft starts sobbing when I tell her it's me. "Eee, lass, where are you? I've been upturned and wondering if someone'll find you under a motorcar's wheels."

My heart stops. She can't know. I've never told anyone about my mom.

"I'm safe."

I can hear her blow her nose. "Mrs. Brumpton called on the telephone too."

"Called? From the ship?" Mrs. Meadowcroft must have got it wrong. I know I'm not up to the minute on my 1912 technology, but I'm pretty sure Mrs. Brumpton can't telephone the house from the ship.

"No, lass. She called to say they've had motorcar trouble and they've missed the *Titanic*."

"That's great!" The hotel clerk looks up. She's listening to my conversation, and I turn the other way.

"You'll miss them, is that why?" Mrs. Meadowcroft asks. "But they're still going, lass."

"How?"

"They're boarding tomorrow. In Ireland."

"Ireland!"

"Aye. Mrs. Brumpton said today the ship stops in France. Then tomorrow 'tis Queenstown, Ireland."

I close my eyes. Queenstown. Ireland. Tomorrow. There's still time to save the Brumptons. Then I remember and open my eyes. "But Adrian. He's on the *Titanic* on his own."

"Eee, lass."

"I have to get a message to him."

There's a pause, then she says, "You could send him a Marconigram."

"Marconigram?" I ask, vaguely remembering the name from history class a long time ago.

"Wireless message," Mrs. Meadowcroft answers. "I read

about them in the newspaper. When are you coming back? We miss you, lass."

"Soon." Perhaps there's still a chance Adrian and me can make it down the dumbwaiter, after all. "When are you closing the house?"

"We're getting it ready now."

I sigh. So much for my so-called life.

"Do you know where the Brumptons are right now? I've got to tell them not to get on that ship."

"They're waiting for their motor to be repaired. I don't know the name of the place, but I think Mrs. B. said it was close to the train station. But Sally, you can't tell your betters what they can and cannot do. Best come home."

I shake my head, too tired to argue with her 1912 rules. "Do you know how long their car will take to repair?"

"All day, Mrs. Brumpton said."

"Thanks. Don't worry, I'll see you soon."

Putting the phone on its hook, I ask the hotel clerk for the place to send a Marconigram, and she directs me to a building on Canute Road.

"I've got a brother working on the *Titanic,*" she says, proudly.

I can't look her in the face. So I thank her for the use of the phone and get out of there, pronto.

With a burst of energy, I hurry through the crowded streets of Southampton, deciding at the last moment to jump onto a passing tram.

I climb upstairs and sit up top. As the tram sways and rumbles along, I glance at the empty seat next to me. The seat Adrian should be in. I've really messed things up coming to 1912. I have to put them right.

WARNING

CANUTE CHAMBERS the name above the three curved windows says. And on the door: White Star Office—MARCONI OPERATOR ON DUTY. I climb three steps, straighten my hat, check to see my coat loops are fastened, and push open the door.

There's a desk clerk with big square shoulders, standing behind the counter.

Trying to act confident, I stride up and say, "I need to send a Marconigram to the *Titanic*."

"Well," the clerk says, resting his elbow on the counter. "If the operator could get the thing working." He half turns his big shoulders to speak to the thinnest man I've ever seen, sitting at a desk fiddling with coils and dials. "That right there, Arthur?"

The clerk turns back to me with a look that says Arthur's useless. "We've had people in all day wanting to send messages to the *Titanic*—toffs mostly," he says.

I nod as if I understand what toffs mean.

"Hey, Arthur," the clerk shouts. "You've got a mate working on the *Titanic*, haven't you?"

The skinny Arthur answers without lifting his eyes from his Marconi message machine.

"That's right—Harold Bride—I could do with him here to help me fix this thing. Instead he's travelling the world."

"Yes," the clerk says to me, "Arthur went to the Marconi School with Harold, but Harold's the lucky one, off on a fancy ship." He stretches out the word fancy.

"Tell you what," the clerk says, winking down at me. "Let me write your message, just in case miracles happen and he gets it working." He picks up a pencil and poises it over a message slip. "Who's it going to?"

I look down at the message slip. "To Adrian Merryweather. Manservant to the Brumpton family of Robin Hood's Bay, Yorkshire, England."

"To save you money," the helpful clerk suggests, "let's just write Manservant to the Brumptons."

"Thanks." I pause, realizing I don't know how to word a Marconigram. I close my eyes trying to dig deep for a movie from the black-and-white days.

"It's just like sending a telegram," the clerk says. Which makes *It's a Wonderful Life* come to me because George Bailey receives a telegram at the end of the movie. How does it go? Mr. (someone) cables you need cash. STOP. My office instructed to advance you up to twenty (something) thousand dollars. STOP.

I clear my throat. "Family not on board. STOP. Get off ship before it sinks. STOP. Just do it. STOP. Sally."

The clerk throws his pencil down and it bounces off the desk. "Sinks! You need to get out of here. Now!"

For the first time the skinny one, Arthur, looks up from his Marconi machine and stares at me with sad, suffering eyes.

"Get back to work, you," the clerk snaps at him.

All the disappointment of the day wells up inside me. "I can send whatever message I like," I shout.

The big-shouldered clerk narrows his eyes. "Who d'you really work for? Cunard? Trying to cause a scare are you?"

He strides out from behind the desk, hunching those shoulders, ape-like, as he goes to push me from the building.

I don't give him the chance. With one glance at the astonished Arthur, I exit the White Star offices, tripping down the front steps on the way.

"And don't come back," I can hear the clerk call after me. "Or I'll set the law on ya."

Running from the building, holding onto my hat, I don't stop until I reach the end of the road.

Now I rest, leaning on a castle-type wall. Trying to get my energy back. Trying to stop the shaking in my legs.

Clutching a painful stitch in my side, I wonder why I'm in 1912, because nothing I've done has made a difference. Not my conversations with Mrs. Brumpton and Lydia, not the phone call from the Robin Hood Inn, not the trip down to the docks. Nothing. And now I can't even send Adrian a Marconigram.

Maybe I'll have more luck with finding the family.

I push down my feelings of panic and turn and limp towards the train station where the garage that's fixing their car is supposed to be close to.

LAST CHANCE

The garage, two blocks down at the back of the train station, is dark and dirty. But a single electric light bulb glows over the engine of a black car and, stood to one side, a mechanic listens with his ear to the motor.

I look around like crazy for any sign of the Brumptons. They're just leaving, the mechanic tells me when I ask. Car's already fixed. He points the way, and I can't believe my luck. I have to get to them.

Tires are stacked next to the wall, and a heavy looking metal crowbar is lying on the oily ground. I jump over it, skidding on the oil, and dash through the open doors at the back of the garage.

Mr. Brumpton's nail-polish red car is just turning into the road!

As if directed by an invisible movie director, I leap forward, waving my arms about. Mr. Brumpton's car skids and swerves sideways.

* * *

They all climb out.

Mr. Brumpton.

Mrs. Brumpton.

Lydia.

Mr. Brumpton shouts, "Are you stark staring mad, girl, running into the road like that?" He doesn't recognize me, and I stupidly start brushing down the front of my dark green coat to impress him.

"Mr. Brumpton. It's me. Sally. Your maid."

He tilts his head and recognizes me. "What's happened at the house?"

"Your house is—nothing, nothing." The lie about the fire is just way too big. I can't pull it off.

"Sally," Mrs. Brumpton says. "Why are you here? Oh, your family live in Southampton, don't they?"

"Umm, well, no." And I feel like we're chatting in the morning room instead of in the middle of the road in Southampton.

It's quiet, traffic-wise, but Mr. Brumpton's sideways car is attracting people passing.

"I had to stop you."

"What?" Mr. Brumpton asks me.

"I came to stop you getting on the *Titanic*."

He frowns. "Mrs. Brumpton told me you were dead against it. You're not still going down that track?"

I nod, not knowing what else to say. I'm about to plead with Mrs. Brumpton and Lydia but they're looking up at Mr. Brumpton, respectfully waiting. I realize I need to convince him. The 1912 man of the house. It's my only chance.

"Hasn't Mrs. Brumpton given you a good home?" he says. "Overlooked your shortcomings? Treated you like family?"

I stare at the road between us. If he climbs back in his car now and decides to leave for the *Titanic* I'll have to tell him I'm from the future.

"Well?" he asks.

I can't tell him in the middle of the road. In front of all these people now milling round in front of Mrs. Brumpton and Lydia.

"Can we go somewhere quiet and talk?"

"No," he says.

I look straight into his eyes, and for the first time I see Gran's blue eyes staring back. The world around me fades, and I'm ready to talk, but he's turned away and is stepping towards his car. "Just listen to me," I call out in frustration. "Just this once, listen." I have a moment of inspiration. "Edison. Imagine I'm Thomas Edison."

He turns around.

I stop shouting and try to keep my voice calm. "I don't expect you to understand. But in a few days the *Titanic* will sink. You'll pick up your newspaper and read the headlines and you'll think about it for the rest of your life. People will talk about it for the rest of your life. I can't stop the *Titanic*. I would if I could. But I can stop you. So, please, please, listen."

He turns and walks away.

I can't stop him. I have no control. The tears are rolling down my cheeks. "Adrian's on the ship. You have to get Adrian off that ship."

Mr. Brumpton is shaking his head. I can't stand it. Why doesn't he stop shaking his head? I have to stop him. I run over to the garage and pick up the crowbar. I don't remember running back into the road, but I'm hitting his car. Smashing it. Hitting the lamps. Hitting the engine. Breaking the glass. I'm killing the car. The car kills people. It killed my mom. I'd have had a mom if it wasn't for the car. Smash. Crunch. Smash. Crunch. Again and again and again.

A hand pulls my collar back.

In slow motion, I let the crowbar slip. Something inside me breaks. I lie very still, curled up in ball with the sky pressing down; I'm in a box of air, fighting for breath, and the ground spins and spins and spins again until I want it to spin me home. I can't act in this movie. Not now, not never.

"Are you responsible for her?" a man's voice asks.

"We have a ship to board," Mr. Brumpton's voice says.

"We can't just leave her here," Mrs. Brumpton's voice says.

If I could just go to sleep right here.

Mr. Brumpton pulls my arm.

"The dumbwaiter worked, Mr. Brumpton," I manage to say. "The dumbwaiter worked. Edison's machine worked." I look up. "You're not Mr. Brumpton." I'm staring at the policeman from the docks. He lifts me off the ground.

"She's being arrested, mother" Lydia yells. "Do something."

I feel myself floating. The crowd presses in. I'm half walked, half carried away. But I hear their voices:

Don't let her lose her hat.

Is she a suffragette?

She won't get the vote doing that.

Is she dangerous?

Did you see that motorcar? It'll never work again.

Who is she?

She's a suffragette.

They'll force feed her, then.

Only if she refuses to eat.

What's that? She's starving?

Yes. That's why she bashed that rich person's motorcar in.

And as I float away, I can't shake the idea I've lost Adrian. On a ship I knew was going to sink. How terrible that I let it happen. I stood there and watched him get on, knowing the ocean will swallow it up. That all its shiny plates will smash. That one of its towering funnels will fall. That all its lights will go out.

I stood there and let him go on.

ARRESTED

I'm afraid to open my eyes. I've been processed they say, days ago, and I'm lying in a long ward with stark white walls. Apart from the rows of beds and a stern-faced nurse writing at a desk at the end of the room, you wouldn't even know this was a hospital. There are no heart monitors, no tubes, no beeping machines hooked-up to patients.

There are doctors, though. One saw me on his rounds today. He wore a white coat that flapped along as he walked. He said I could end up in a borstal—a prison for children. "I may have to stand up and give evidence on your behalf. Is your mistress kind? Does she give you regular meals?" He said he was impressed with my teeth.

Another doctor came after that, but he wasn't wearing a white coat. He spoke with a soft voice and wanted to know how long I've been seeing cameras following me around. He made some notes when I told him ever since I arrived in 1912.

I've lost my job. Birkett would be happy.

The Brumptons? They went to America on another ship.

At least I did one thing right.

* * *

Days later, I wake up but my eyes are still closed. I can hear doctors working on the next patient. There's a terrible gassy smell in the air that makes me see the color purple for some reason. I clutch at my cold sheet and pull it under my nose. The nurse is here now and her voice is so strict I have to open my eyes.

"If you think it's hard being a servant you should try being a nurse. Pull yourself together, snap out of it, we need the bed."

"I'm free to leave?"

"Yes. So get dressed." She holds out my clothes, all neatly folded like a gift.

"What about borstal?"

"All charges dropped."

Charges dropped. Why?

A shiver creeps up through my body and runs down my spine. The news has hit that the *Titanic* has sunk.

I know it.

WHICH WAY?

I'm being escorted from the hospital, and my legs are trembling on the way down the stairs to the front door. On the street outside, I don't know which way to turn. I fasten my dark green coat and set off down the empty street. The clouds are low in the sky. Pressing down.

I rest at the town clock, then turn a corner and find myself on Canute Road. It's filled with people gathering outside the White Star office, where I tried to send the Marconigram. Cars are arriving; their drivers park where they stop, at any angle. A horse waits patiently next to its coachman.

I hover on the edge of the crowd and start talking to a lady in a worn black coat. She reminds me of Mrs. Meadowcroft. The lady's son is on the *Titanic*, a fireman from the engine room, she tells me, and she's waiting for news. An important looking man told her the ship was still afloat, on it's way to Halifax in Canada with every soul safe. "It can't have sunk," she says. "He's getting married. I've got him a pair of good shoes, so he can go to the dance with his girl."

I look down at the ground and start biting my nails.

People stride in and out of the White Star office. Men, mostly. The crowd is full of women, some holding babies, and they talk together, whispering in small groups. I stay here all day. When it's dark someone hangs lanterns next to a bulletin board. Names are posted. Black ink. Letters three inches deep.

The crowd is silent.

Then. "Thank God. Thank God," a woman shouts.

Pushing forward, I scour the survivors' list.

Adrian's name is not there.

FIRST CLASS

Time creeps by. Like someone's superglued the hands of the town clock down. I wander the streets, passing the castle-type wall, the docks, The Dolphin hotel where I used the telephone. I go in the hotel and call Brumpton Manor. The phone rings and rings and rings.

I sleep on a bench, making a pillow out of a folded newspaper. In the dawn a policeman moves me on. I run away, afraid he'll arrest me.

At a tea wagon, the lady serving tells me I've newspaper ink on my face. I leave it there as I sip my tea. Across the road a newspaper boy is shouting the sad news. He looks happy because his papers are selling fast.

* * *

The next day I go back to The Dolphin. And the next. I read the newspaper there. It's filled with stories of first-class passengers. Of private trains ready to take rich women home. Of brave rich men. Of cowardly rich men. What about the crew? The ordinary passengers? The servants?

It's warm in this hotel, and I fall asleep in a low-lit corner of the lobby in a soft chair with a fat velvet cushion. I wake up when a bellboy passes me my hat off the floor. For a second I think it's Adrian. But this boy is not as tall and has black hair. The hotel is busy, and he rushes off.

I fix my hair in the washroom and wipe down my coat. Now I splash my face with water, and wonder why I'm never hungry. I must force myself to eat. All this waiting is driving me nuts. I'm not a waiting type of person. Not any more.

I should go back to Robin Hood's Bay. It makes more sense. Before they realize I'm not a guest here.

At the entrance, I fix my hat and take one last look at The Dolphin before heading towards the train station.

The ticket man takes my last coins.

I turn right. I can't believe my eyes, there's a boy on the floor, hunched over against a wall. He's dirty, scruffy. But I'd know that curly hair anywhere.

ADRIAN'S BACK STORY

Adrian leaps up. I don't know whether to cry or laugh. Instead I scream and run over.

"I thought you'd drowned." I take in his gray eyes. His curls. His long lashes. And now I do cry. He holds onto me, which is just as well as my legs are Jell-O.

He brushes his eyes with the back of his hands. "They wouldn't let me in to see you. I've been waiting here for two days because a policeman moved me on. But I kept going back to the hospital anyway, just in case."

I can only shake my head.

"Let's go home," he murmers. And he puts his arm round my shoulder.

In a daze I watch as he buys his ticket.

We wait for the train. TITANIC SUNK a newspaper board on the platform across the tracks says. APPALLING LOSS OF LIFE another announces.

"You're shivering," Adrian says.

The train pulls in. I don't argue as he helps me on.

* * *

ADRIAN'S BACK STORY

"How?" I simply ask.

Adrian throws his cap on the luggage rack and flops into his seat. "I got your Marconigram."

"Marconigram? But it was never sent."

The train speeds up and we leave Southampton behind.

"The desk clerk at the White Star office said I was a troublemaker. He threw me out."

"Well, someone sent it."

I try to think back. It feels such a long time ago. The day I tried to send the Marconigram. There was the ape-man desk clerk with big shoulders. And the skinny operator—Arthur—that's right. He was trying to fix his machine. Looking at me with his big sad eyes. He must have taken pity on me and sent my Marconigram when he could. Maybe he was getting back at the desk clerk. Whatever the reason: Thank you, Arthur, I have Adrian back.

I try to smile. "I didn't know how long I needed to wait for you. Maybe till I was all cobwebby like old Miss Havisham in *Great Expectations*."

"Hey, I know that one." Adrian shakes his head. "I don't usually understand half the stuff you say."

"Ditto."

He looks serious for a second. "The Brumptons?" he asks.

"Safe."

He nods his head and sighs. He looks zonked.

"I got off at France."

"France!"

He offers me a piece of French candy, as if to prove it. "Aye. I had no brass, so I was stuck. It's taken me all this time to get back."

"How did you do it?"

"I worked in the fields for some farmers till they paid me—but I did manage to pick up me watch." He holds up his golden pocket watch and his eyes shine as he dangles it on its chain. He goes quiet for a second. "It wasn't good in France."

"It wasn't good here." I gaze out the train window. The back yards of the row houses speed by. "How did you know where I was?"

"When I got onto English soil, I called the house. Mrs. Meadowcroft answered. She told me where you were. She didn't believe it, though." He leans forward. "Did you really wreck their new motorcar?"

I shake my head to let him know I'm not ready to talk about it yet. One day soon, I'll tell him about my mom.

For the rest of the train journey we catch up. But at the back of my mind, all the time I'm thinking—closed house or not, we can try to get to my time now.

Back to Gran.

ROBIN HOOD'S BAY

Yes, it's true. The house is closed. Locked up.

But Uncle Thaddeus is home.

We drink tea in his little cottage and he tells us the other servants have found places to stay. Like Old Jack who is living at Boggle Hole with Copper. And Ned who is gardening for the Whitby mayor. Gerty is with her big family. And Mrs. Meadowcroft's gone away to her sister's in Jersey. Not New Jersey in my America, but the one in the Channel Islands, near France.

I wish she were here.

We move into the cottage. Uncle Thaddeus is a quiet man for someone so tall. I soon get used to the hole in his tooth where his pipe rests. He and Adrian sleep on the squashy chairs downstairs. I sleep in the loft with the window nudged open, so I can hear the sea.

The other servants visit. "What happened in Southampton?" they ask. "How did you know the *Titanic* would sink?" Some of them even want me to read their tealeaves. "Would you describe the man I'm going to marry?" Gerty begs. "And does he look like the milkman?"

I just smile and look over at Adrian. He doesn't smile back.

For a couple of days people in the village shake his hand or pat him on the back. He says he's never known anything like it. I tell him he's famous now, having escaped a big disaster.

After a while though, the novelty wears off and people just wave. At the end of the week they're down to just nodding.

I keep waiting for Adrian to mention the dumbwaiter or the key crystal or anything to do with time travel. He's gone quiet since coming back from France. Maybe he's waiting for me.

Right, then. Today's the day.

* * *

But we have to help his uncle clean his boat. The sun's setting on the sea when I get the chance.

"Let's go see Smudge," I suggest. Adrian's been popping into the Brumptons' garden to feed him scraps.

"We can break a window and climb into the house," I tell him, when we reach the donkey path. "I don't know why I didn't think of it before."

Adrian doesn't look so sure.

I argue my case. "But we have to go before the Brumptons come back and start asking awkward questions."

Adrian finally speaks. But really quietly. "What would you say to Mr. Brumpton if he asked how you knew the *Titanic* would sink?"

"There's no need to tell him I'm from the future. I don't have to save his family now. But, Adrian, don't you get it? There's no need to talk to the Brumptons at all, if we just go to my time."

I steer him towards the direction of the house, and start going on about America. How one day we'll make it to the theme parks. How he'll get a kick out the rides. "We'll get weekend jobs and save the money," I tell him, planning our future. Then I have a light-bulb moment. "When we're older, we can even get a job in a theme park."

I picture us inside Magic Kingdom, helping a little kid onto a ride. It feels great. The feeling. "It won't be a career. Just a summer job, maybe. Or a student job." And instead of Orlando being a place locked out to me, it now feels like a place to get excited about. To be proud of. And I can't stop smiling as I think of us having fun together. "I want to go to Hollywood Studios first, then Islands of Adventure, then we can go to Epcot where there's all these replica countries and you can tell me, 'We're travelling the world.' "

"Stop!" he shouts.

I stop. Literally. And a horrible thought tunnels its way into my brain. "You're coming back with me, right? Friends for life?"

"No," he says in a ghost of a voice.

* * *

"What!"

I try to control the desperation in my own voice. "After everything we've been through. What've you got to lose? Apart from a run-around job? And an uncle who's away at sea most the time?"

We've reached Brumpton Manor, and Adrian gazes up at the big house. "I know, but—"

I don't let him finish. "You're always saying how great it'd be to live in my time."

He shakes his head. It feels like a punch in the stomach.

I pull him round to face me. "I won't be able to come back. I live in Orlando. That's thousands of miles away from the dumbwaiter. One shot. Adrian. I've got one shot."

He leans his back against a tree and looks ahead, turning his watch over and over in his hand. I follow his gaze. He's looking at the circle of red roofs that make up Robin Hood's

Bay. I try to get his attention, but he *will not* look at my face. I know now that the decision's too hard. That he can never leave his village. His home.

"I just . . . I just thought we'd be together. Always."

He doesn't answer but he presses in my hand the heart-shaped halfpenny he always keeps in his pocket for good luck.

A cold wind shivers in the trees. Adrian pulls away from the tree, and I follow him to the house. We can hear Smudge meowing from behind the garden wall.

He opens the gate and walks through. But all I see through my tears is his silhouette; Smudge at his feet, just a blur.

CRYSTAL POWER

Uncle Thaddeus goes back to sea. For days I try to carry on as usual. Putting off what I know I must do. I've still not given up on persuading Adrian, though he's given up on telling me why not. Either way, something happens that pushes me to try to get to my time.

The Brumptons have sent word they're coming back.

* * *

All today I've gone about the village in a dream state, hardly saying anything to Adrian. My plans are made. There's no choice now that I know the Brumptons could arrive any time soon.

It's night now, and the cottage windows twinkle with candlelight. Like shadows we walk past the Lifeboat House, listening to the wind blowing the sea on the cliffs. The sky's clear and the stars seem close, though I know they must be light years away.

We turn towards the donkey path without saying a word.

There's not a single person left in the house. Everything's closed up. But I'm afraid to go in right now. I'm afraid to let this night ever end.

Adrian helps me break a kitchen window, and as I carefully climb in, I silently thank the stars Birkett's no longer around to ruin my plan.

He lights me a lamp, and we climb to the top of our stairs to my attic room. To grab Edison's papers. And I remember the night I fell down the dumbwaiter and we walked up these stairs. My legs are stronger. I can keep up with him now.

Downstairs, the kitchen's quiet except for the ticking clock. Smudge is warm in my bed. I half wish I was with him. What if something goes wrong? And once I'm gone from 1912, I'm gone for good. The whole thing feels so final.

"Are you ready?" Adrian whispers.

Heart thumping, I close my eyes and nod.

He passes me his lantern and climbs into the chute to lift the dumbwaiter's trapdoor. Scratching at the sparkling soil, he exposes the key crystal. Wow. It never fails to amaze me.

I read out Edison's instructions, one-by-one.

Adrian checks each cog and lever. "Hold that lantern up, will you?"

"Let's set the date," I tell him, and a shiver of electricity runs down my spine.

"Not yet," he says.

"Set it." And I sound like Abigail when she doesn't want to scrub floors.

"No."

My sadness at him for not wanting to leave 1912 turns to anger. "First you won't come with me, now you won't set the date."

He straightens up and climbs out the dumbwaiter chute. "You set it."

"I will, then," I say to his back.

But I sense him hovering somewhere in the hallway.

I climb into the chute. It's not easy on my own, trying to read Edison's instructions and fiddle with the settings.

Thanks Adrian, for nothing.

But when I'm finished, and I see him sitting on the stone steps, his hands holding his head, I can't be mad.

"Let's go," I whisper.

* * *

Three times I change my mind. But no matter how long I wait, it feels like I'm leaving too soon. Only the thought of Gran waiting persuades me now.

Shaking, I take off my coat. I'm wearing my nightgown and robe. I don't want to explain to anyone in my time about my uniform dress.

I take one last look at my lovely coat.

Throwing off my boots, I climb into the dumbwaiter in the dining room and curl up like a ball.

Adrian has gone to the kitchen to start the dumbwaiter there. He says he can't say goodbye and he can't watch me go. But that's not right. Saying goodbye is important.

Deep down, though, I understand. I can't face never seeing him again, either, because all my life I've wanted a friend. A proper I-can-tell-you-anything friend. But the theme park thing got in the way. The money thing. But here it doesn't matter. Here in 1912 there are no theme parks. Adrian doesn't care about the newest technology, the latest clothes, the nicest house with screened-in pool. And now, somewhere in time, he'll be living his life without me. Missing.

"'Bye, Adrian," I say in my head. "'Bye, 1912."

I shift my position in the dumbwaiter, trying to avoid the rough spot. A rumbling noise breaks the silence of the house, and I want to scream. What if it breaks? What if I'm trapped? Or I end up missing forever? I grip onto the sides. This time there is no other warning.

I just plummet down the chute and spin.

FRANTIC

I tumble out the dumbwaiter and grip my knee in pain, rocking from side to side on the cold, smooth floor. Bright lights switch on, and I cover my eyes.

"Sally! Sally! Are you OK?" Gran takes hold of my arms.

I scream. But not because of my knee.

"Oh my God, is something broken?"

I can't speak.

"What happened?" I hear a woman's voice say and wonder whose it is.

"I don't know, Dottie."

That's who. My second aunt once removed. Aunt Dottie. And I wish she would remove herself so I could have Gran all to myself.

I try to uncover my eyes. "The lights," I whimper. "The lights are too bright."

Aunt Dottie leans over me. "She may have concussion."

"Can you move?" Gran asks, pulling gently on my arm.

I start to cry.

Gran lifts me up. I try to rest my foot down but a deep pain shoots up my leg.

"It's too late for the doctor. I'll get some ice."

Aunt Dottie dashes over to the fridge and, holding a glass

under, presses a button. Ice comes tumbling out. "We may need to get her to the hospital."

"No. No. I'm fine," I lie. I close my eyes and see Adrian's face.

Gran lowers me carefully onto a kitchen stool. "Why were you wandering about in the dark? Did you have a nightmare?"

I shake my head and grab hold of Gran and hug and hug and hug her.

"Well," Aunt Dottie says, icing my knee. "That's a fine start to your holiday."

TELL ME

Torn ligaments the doctor said, and I'm all bandaged up. Last night Gran and Aunt Dottie helped me into bed, given me two painkillers, and I'd slept soundly, exhaustion grabbing hold of me and knocking me out.

Now I'm in Aunt Dottie's basement living room; my leg propped up on a footstool. I keep looking round for all the other servants.

"Was it the jet lag?" Gran asks, smoothing down her color-clashing orange and red skirt.

I love it.

"Was what the jet lag?"

"Why you hurt yourself in the middle of the night."

"It was something lag," I tell her. I look at her face. I feel as if I've changed but she hasn't.

She frowns. "Jet lag must be unsettling. I had a dream you were missing." She stares at me. "It was so vivid."

I lean over and give her a hug—as if I'm the parent—and she smiles.

I settle back into my chair. There's no view from this window, not of Robin Hood's Bay. Just worn-down steps going up to the scullery yard that Aunt Dottie now calls the patio. The old mangle and washing line are gone, replaced with garden furniture and brightly painted pots of plants and growing bulbs. I liked the scullery yard better before.

Gerty was in that one.

I glance at the door. I can hear Aunt Dottie in her kitchen rattling around. She just did the laundry in forty minutes flat. After that, the vacuuming, and I'd stared at her cleaner in envy as it smartly sucked the dirt up. I've asked her all sorts of vague questions about the dumbwaiter. I can tell she doesn't have a clue. Or she's a good actress.

Like me.

I look at Gran's face. I can't get enough of it. I'm used to keeping secrets but every cell in my body now screams to tell her about the things I've seen and done. The things I know.

"Anyroad, Gran."

"Anyroad? That's a funny thing to say."

"Just something I heard ... in a movie. So, anyroad, tell me about my ancestors. Tell me all you know."

Aunt Dottie pushes through the living-room door, carrying a tray with her golden mugs on and a packet of chocolate cookies. "You look surprised," she says to Gran. "How come?"

"Sally's just asked me to tell her about our ancestors. She never has before."

Aunt Dottie places the tray down. It's lined with a Robin Hood's Bay tea towel, and I feel like showing her where Uncle Thaddeus's cottage is.

"I'll get my photographs out, if you like," Aunt Dottie says. "May as well, seeing as you're stuck here."

I lean forward to reach for a cookie.

"Ouch," I say, gripping my knee. "That'd be great."

Gran gives my knee a worried look.

But Aunt Dottie stares at my hair. I think she's going to mention the color again but she says, "Have you put extensions in this morning?"

"Umm, no." I flip my hair back. I washed it over the sink. I think I used a whole bottle of shampoo.

"It looks longer. Must be because you washed it. Anyway, I'll get those photos." She turns to Gran. I can make coffee if you like, but we Brits, we love our tea."

"I know someone British who doesn't like tea," I mumble.

"What?" Aunt Dottie asks.

"Nowt."

She arches an eyebrow.

"Nothing."

Family Photos

Lydia standing on the front steps between
Mr. and Mrs. Brumpton.

Mr. Brumpton leaning against a new silver car.

Mrs. Brumpton glancing back at the house.

Lydia carrying a Votes-for-Women banner.

So Lydia joined the suffragettes, after all.

I smile.

Pointing to her, I say to Gran, "This is Lydia Brumpton, right? What relation is she to me?"

"She'll be your great-great-grandmother," Gran says, looking pleased.

"That makes Mrs. Brumpton my great-great-great-grandmother. And Mr. Brumpton—"

"That's right, your great-great-great-grandfather, Philip Brumpton." Gran's on a roll. I guess she's enjoying my attention at last.

She points to the photograph of Mr. Brumpton leaning against his car. It isn't the car I smashed. "That's a Silver Ghost Rolls-Royce," she tells me. "Amazing, isn't it?"

It *was* amazing. An even better car than he had before.

Gran points to Mrs. Brumpton.

"That's Kate Brumpton. All I know about her is she was a generous woman."

Mrs. B. was many things, but . . . generous? "In what way?"

"They say," Aunt Dottie says, "for the first half of her life she was careful with her money. But something happened—I don't know what it was but it totally changed her and she started giving her servants top wages—for the times, anyway."

Something happened. Well, I think I can guess what it was.

"Plus," Gran adds, "she always had servants. Even when it wasn't the fashion."

"Gran"—for some reason I can't stop saying her name—"did you meet Lydia? She was your . . . what was she to you?"

"Lydia Brumpton was my grandmother, but I never met her. Or I don't remember—I was just a baby when she died."

"She died? . . . Yes, of course, she died." And I shiver.

"But what a life," Gran adds. "Fighting for women's rights. She was involved in the unions too. Workers' safety conditions and all that."

"Yes," Aunt Dottie says, joining in. "She had meetings in this very house." She looks around. "It used to be the servants' quarters down here, you know; this was part of the kitchen. When we renovated, we had to pull out a big old black cooking range. The coal type." Aunt Dottie nods at me. "They never had electricity in this village until 1932. Imagine that the next time you're plugging in your hair dryer."

"And imagine all the work to heat this place," Gran adds. "Running up and down stairs with coal buckets all day."

"Yes," Aunt Dottie says. "I hope you know you're very lucky, Sally. Never having to do that."

I start to laugh.

They look at me with their mouths open, but I can't stop.

"Well, what's got into her?" Aunt Dottie says.

Gran holds a photo up to try and shut me up.

"Look. Sally. Here's a photograph of all the servants who used to work here."

I stop laughing.

Gran flips the photo over and reads the writing on the back. "*'Brumpton Manor Servants 1912.'*" She passes it over.

I stare at us all lined up. I'm standing next to Adrian. His curls are flattened down for the photo. He makes me smile.

"Don't they look serious?" Gran says. "Except for that maid who's smiling."

I can't believe Gran doesn't recognize me. It makes me feel all time-travel weird.

"Do you know what happened to any of them?" I ask.

"Not really," Aunt Dottie says. "Servants were just there to work. No one cared about their actual lives."

"I thought you knew something about her." Gran points to Abigail. "Wasn't she famous or something?"

"Famous? Oh, yes, you're right. I'd forgotten. Abigail Wainwright. Or Lady Abbey Wright, actress and cousin to the King, as she was known locally. Not proper fame. But enough to get her noticed by the West End. But she ruined it all. Lying about her identity. She wasn't a proper lady and a friend of hers she'd double-crossed let the cat out of the bag and she became a bit of a joke."

Now why doesn't that surprise me?

"And look," Gran adds. "A real cat's walked into the photograph."

Aunt Dottie leans over to see. "So it has." She takes the photo off me. "That reminds me. When your Mum and Dad were staying here—"

"They stayed here!"

"Yes. A sort of honeymoon, though they'd been married

a while. Anyway, your mum found a stray kitten. Wanted to take it back to America."

"Oh?" Gran says.

"Yes. I told them it wasn't practical, but they wouldn't listen. Your Dad had to go through all this fuss, getting it a health certificate, putting its name on its collar." Aunt Dottie shakes her head.

Gran coughs her nervous cough. "You never said."

"It doesn't matter," Aunt Dottie says. "It disappeared."

"Do you remember, what name?" I ask as the room spins. "What name did Mom call the cat?" But I knew before she told me.

"Smudge."

NO MORE TIME

I've figured something out. Today—May 16th—is Adrian's fifteenth birthday. Not today here. Here it's still February. But today if I were back in time.

Will anyone buy him a present?

Do they do that for servants in Robin Hood's Bay?

In 1912?

I haven't seen the village. Not down here with my bad knee. And I don't have a wheelchair. There's no way Aunt Dottie or Gran can push one up and down Bay's steep steps. It's been seven days now. Soon, I think I'll go nuts if I don't get out of this basement. And tomorrow we're going back to Orlando.

Gran's out with Aunt Dottie. They've gone on a bus tour but didn't want to go without me. I insisted. Bad knee or no bad knee, I've got something I need to do. I want to see the village one more time.

From my attic room.

* * *

NO MORE TIME

They're still here. Our servants' stairs. I start the slow climb up, heaving my bandaged knee, one step at a time. At each landing window I plan to stop and rest and soak up the view.

I reach the first landing window. I can see the stables. They've been converted into garages. No Old Jack. No Copper. "Machines don't have hearts," I hear Old Jack say, and my own heart hurts.

At the next landing, I see the meadows rising gently up and down. They haven't been built on. Phew. But I still can't see the village. Not from this side of the house.

At the next window, I look at the tree I wanted to climb down on my first day in 1912—I lean against the window and look up—the tree's taller now.

I'm nearly at the top. I think I'm making my knee worse. I hold onto the next window and wait for the pain to go away.

One more set of stairs. I stop and rest my knee again. What if my room's locked? What if it's not there any more? Converted into something for Aunt Dottie's hotel.

Now I'm at the top. I look at the long hallway of closed doors. I've been in most of these rooms.

Gerty's: Bare as if she's never in it.

Abigail's: Tidy. Photos on the wall of 1912 actors. One of the Electric Theater where they show silent movies.

I hobble past and stop at Mrs. Meadowcroft's room. Once, I'd opened her door and stared round with my mouth open. Everywhere was covered in half-finished paintings of Robin Hood's Bay. Not in a hundred years would I have guessed Mrs. Meadowcroft was an artist.

"Painting brushes the loneliness away," she'd told me later.

I start limping again.

There's the skylight. But no table piled high with clean sheets. No clock to remind me it's time for work.

My door's not locked. Just jammed. My heart starts

thumping as I push and push until there's enough space for me to squeeze through.

My room is stacked with old stuff that wasn't old last week. There's my wardrobe straight out of Narnia, and my bed, piled high with curled-up car magazines and cracked gramophone records.

I edge towards the window, squeeze past a tea table, and move out of the way a lady figurine with her finger missing. My knee's throbbing, but the pain disappears when I see the view.

The grassy backyard and winding footpath.

The gate.

The donkey path.

I follow the donkey path with my eyes as it slopes off, down to the tight cluster of red-roofed cottages all grouped in a circle next to the sea.

Robin Hood's Bay.

Exactly the same.

Except no Ma Thompson's. No Uncle Thaddeus's cottage.

No Adrian.

He's a hundred years away.

Did I dream the whole thing? I move a lantern to one side and sit down, resting my elbows on the windowsill. And there it is. Cut into the wood:

Sally and Adrian
April 1912

No dream then. No dream.

I turn and drop face down onto the bed, and I cry and cry and cry. With relief at being back with Gran. With grief at what I've left behind.

Pop quiz: Where's *my* Hollywood ending?

I mean, after everything I've been through. Being a maid.

Putting up with Birkett. Running away to the *Titanic*. Running out of money in a creepy town. Being arrested. Nearly losing the Brumptons. Losing Adrian.

I sit up and take his heart-shaped coin from my pocket and roll it between my finger and thumb.

One last look out the window. My window. At the village. Tomorrow I'm losing that too.

The climb back down the servants' stairs, I hardly notice. So lost in my thoughts, I barely feel my knee.

But there in the kitchen, sitting on the floor near the dumbwaiter—is Adrian!

"What?" I want to scream but no sound comes.

He looks up at me, his gray eyes twinkling.

"Happy birthday," I finally manage to whisper.

And he smiles.

ALSO BY CATHERINE HARRIOTT

FICTION
Sally's Movie Diary
A companion to Missing in Time

Film fan Sally Soforth has been though a secret portal where she met Adrian, a boy from the past. Now she's writing this diary to him about the movies she loves and her dreams for the future, but is he really there or does she just wish he was?

NON FICTION
Orlando Tips for Brits
Comprehensive guide for visitors, holiday home investors, and anyone thinking of moving to the Sunshine State

Printed in Great Britain
by Amazon